CENTER STAGE
Bright Lights Billionaire #2
by
ALI PARKER

Table of Contents

Chapter 1.................................4
  Chapter 2................................12
  Chapter 3................................20
  Chapter 4................................29
  Chapter 5................................37
  Chapter 6................................45
  Chapter 7................................52
  Chapter 8................................59
  Chapter 9................................65
  Chapter 10...............................72
  Chapter 11...............................79
  Chapter 12...............................85
  Chapter 13...............................93
  Chapter 14...............................100
  Chapter 15...............................106
  Chapter 16...............................114
  Chapter 17...............................121
  Chapter 18...............................128
  Chapter 19...............................134
  Chapter 20...............................139
  Want more?...............................144
  About the Author.........................145
  Books by Ali.............................146

Baited
Second Chance Romances
Jaded
Justified
Judged
Alpha Billionaire Series
Alpha Billionaire, Book 1
Alpha Billionaire, Book 2
Together Forever
Bad Money Series
Blood Money
Dirty Money
Hard Money
Cash Money
Forbidden Fruit Series
Forgotten Bodyguard
Future Investment
Risky Business
Bright Lights Billionaire
Stage Left
Center Stage
Pro-U Series
Breakaway

Center Stage
Bright Lights Billionaire #2
Copyright © 2016 by Ali Parker
All rights reserved. This book or any portion thereof may not be reproduced or used in any manner whatsoever without the express written permission of the publisher except for the use of brief quotations in a book review.

The novel is a work of fiction. Names, characters, places and plot are all either products of the author's imagination or used fictitiously. Any resemblance to actual events, locales, or persons – living or dead – is purely coincidental.

First Edition.
Editor: Nicole Bailey, Proof Before You Publish
Designer: JS Marx Designs

Chapter 1

Ethan

It had been a little over a week since Riley signed the papers to join me in *Down Low*, and yet the excitement in me hadn't even had a chance to surface yet. A dark depression over all the shit we'd put each other through during the process tainted my resolve to be my normal happy-go-lucky self, but Deza had been working laborious hours to pull me from my funk.

"Stop dilly-dallying and get that streamer up. I swear you're as useless as a vibrator without batteries." She glanced back at me as she tossed her long black hair over her shoulder.

"I'm so much better than a vibrator. You know they say girth is far more of a stimulant than any jerking motion could ever be." I shrugged and tossed the packet of streamers to her, hitting her in the butt with them. "Score."

"Watch it."

"I am, and I sure do love what I see. You've been working out, haven't you?" I slipped my hands into my slacks and moved to the floor-to-ceiling window as I scanned the parking lot.

"You know, I've always wanted to understand better who *they* were." She ignored my come-on and turned, tilting her head to the side a little. She really was stunning in her own way. Darren, or whatever his name was, had to be a complete idiot to let a woman like Deza out of his life.

"Oh, you know, they are the naysayers. They are the counsel of the high and mighty. They are the definers of all things far and wide." I lifted my hands and walked around the room as if trapped in a Shakespearian monologue.

"Why did I ask you? Jeez." She turned and shook her head as I chuckled.

"Really? I thought that was pretty good acting. No?" She ignored me, so I continued. "*They* would have liked it."

"Yes, *they* would."

I hated to change the subject, and it wasn't a smooth transition by any means, but I needed the answer to the burning question inside of me. "How has Riley been?"

"Good. She's juggling a lot, but she's doing it well."

"I'm not surprised." I hadn't spoken to her for the last five days, which was a relief and a bit depressing altogether.

"You're supposed to be mentoring her. Maybe if you could stop thinking with your little head and start thinking with your big one." She chuckled.

I snorted and turned. "Wait a minute. You *want* me to start thinking with my cock now? Have I gotten this backward my whole life? Shit. That would be *so much* easier. Whew. Glad we got that out of the way."

"You're not going to behave today, are you?" She leaned over, grabbed the streamers and tossed them back to me.

"Not a snowball's chance in hell. I feel like I'm on my man-period. It's liable to get ugly up in here." I rolled my shoulders and lifted the package toward her. "What the fuck am I supposed to do with this? You know people don't use streamers unless they're celebrating a small child's birthday."

"You're acting like a small child. Get over yourself and help me, or go find something better to do."

"Like jack-off in the bathroom?" I walked toward the table and laughed as Frank stood in the doorway with his hands on his hips.

"Why do I feel like this isn't a one-time conversation between the two of you?" He shook his head and walked into the room.

"Because, Frank, what you guys don't know is that my agent has been sexually harassing me for years. No matter what we talk about, it always goes back to my dick. She should be fired." I turned to enjoy the look on Deza's face.

Frank patted my back. "I think you're stuck with her, my friend. Besides, no one else would put up with you, your groupies, or your dick for too long."

"Groupies?" I tossed the streamers to him. "Here, help a sister out and put these up."

"You're useless. You know that?" Deza moved past me and popped me in the stomach. "While you are here-"

"Nope. I'm useless, remember?" I dropped down in the chair closest to me and pulled up my phone, scrolling through it until I found the picture of Riley I'd pulled out of my phone's recycling bin like a true addict. She had me by the throat and the balls, and the saddest part was that she didn't know it. Nor would she ever.

I was grateful that it was a picture on my phone that I had and not a printed photograph. The damn thing would be bent and worn out with torn corners, lip marks on her face and the remnants of jizz smeared on the front of it. The very thought of it had a laugh rumbling through my chest where disgust should have been. I was sick, but I was comfortable just being me.

Riley was the center of my desire, and I had little filter to not give into the naughtiest of thoughts when I was alone with her. Well, her picture.

"Are you ever going to come clean on what the fuck happened with you guys the night before she signed?" Frank walked over and dropped a bag of balloons in my lap. "Blow on these."

"Sexual harassment." I tore the bag open and dumped them out beside me. "I'm worth a billion dollars and you guys have me blowing up balloons. What if I inhale too hard and suck one of these fuckers down my throat."

"I'll take the pictures on my phone." Deza glanced up and smiled toward Frank. "You get them on YouTube?"

"Yep, and I'll give him mouth to mouth. He's been looking for a reason to snuggle up to me for years. This could be his big break." Frank wagged his eyebrows at me, getting me back good for the first time in a long time.

"Fuck you both very much." I turned and worked on blowing up a balloon as my thoughts turned back to the sexy librarian-type that would be playing co-star with me in our next film. She'd been given a golden ticket to come live the life that only the bright lights of Hollywood could offer, and I needed to warn her about so many things. Me being one of them.

Having been an actor since I was old enough to talk, I was numbed to the fame and adoration. It was only skin deep or as far as the wad of cash in my pocket would take me anyway. Riley was new to my world though, and as I'd seen many of my cohorts fall face first before the idol of fame, I felt it my duty to warn her. Funny enough, she just didn't seem like the type that would beckon to the siren's call.

"Hey... spill, Mister. Frank ran to get us some coffee." Deza sat down beside me and ran her hand over the top of my back.

I lifted my leg and shook it like a dog might. "That feels good. Scratch my belly and move lower?"

"Gross." She popped me and sat back. "Spill, Ethan. I know you've been struggling with something since she signed the papers. What happened?"

"I already told you, D. Shit. The story doesn't change. She came over for a conversation, I did as you asked and played gentleman. It sucked to not let her see the real me, but obviously *they* prefer the mask." I put another balloon to my lips, blowing hard.

"I don't believe you." She reached out and gripped the balloon, pulling it hard. My hard work deflated before me, and I picked up another and pulled it tight between my fingers before releasing it and laughing as she squealed.

"Look, she wanted something to happen between us, and I sure as fuck did too." I shrugged. "But, you were right. I need to respect her as my co-worker and not give in to the animalistic urge I have to see how far I can press my-"

"Okay." Deza stood up and lifted her hands. "Save it for the screen. I don't want to hear anything else about the shit running laps in your head."

"Just the stuff about you?" I reached out and gripped her hand.

She turned and looked down at me. "Don't hurt her, okay? She's new to all of this, and you don't know her story at all. Rise above your horniness and help a sister out."

"You or her?" I lifted my eyebrow in genuine confusion. I didn't know her story. Hell, I didn't know Deza's it would seem. At twenty-four I was still operating off of a 'me-only' persona. Something inside of me shifted, and I couldn't tell if it were for the better or not.

"Her, you nugget-head." She tugged her hand from mine and popped me in the head. "And don't be telling no one that she tried to kiss you. Lies only hurt the liar."

"What? That's a fucking lie." I chuckled and rubbed my hands over my chest. "She did try to kiss me, and you'd be proud to know that I carefully turned her down."

"Are you serious?" Deza put her hands on her hips and scowled. She was a small fry, a good head and a half shorter than me, and yet she had the ability to make me wiggle in my seat. She was my mother, my sister, and my best friend most days. Seeing that I didn't have any of those things in my life, she was keeping up quite well.

"Yes." I shrugged and stood up, not liking the way she hovered above me. "She said she was just *testing me* with the kiss thing. I guess she wanted to make sure I wasn't the total cock everyone believes me to be."

"You're not a cock, and no one believes that you are but you." Frank walked back into the room and rolled his eyes. "People are just personifying James Bond onto you."

"Testing you?" Deza seemed to ignore Frank's comment.

I didn't mind so much if people's perception came directly from my on-screen roles, but that wasn't the case at all. I'd been a cock in public in my late teen years, and it'd been a hard pull to get back on track... while faking it.

"Yep." I walked toward the door. "I'm going to get something to drink. I'll be back when the party starts."

"Don't be late." Frank glanced over his shoulder as Deza walked toward me.

"I'll walk you to the elevator." She moved past me into the hall, surprising me a little.

"I'm a big boy now. I even put on my own undies today, the right side out." I wagged my eyebrows at her. "Wanna see?"

"No, pain in my ass, I don't." She slipped her arm into mine and glanced up at me. "I don't think that Riley was testing you for a minute. She's a very straightforward girl, and if she wants to know something, I believe she would just ask."

"Then what do you think she was up to? Trying to sexually harass me in my weakened state?" I pressed the back of my fingers to my head as we stopped by the elevator.

"I swear you're bi-polar."

"Tri... but what's new."

"She has feelings for you." Deza shrugged as if her words didn't mean much.

"Already? Impossible. She doesn't even know me." I reached out and pressed the button on the wall in front of me as I let out a yawn.

"Of course she knows you, Ethan. She's been watching you grow up on screen for the last ten years. We all know you, or think we do." She patted my back as I walked into the elevator and turned around to face her.

"Right... You guys know Ethan Lewis, the actor, but you don't know me."

"I do, sugar cakes."

"This is true, and you're still around. Sounds like you need a raise." I gave her a weak smile as the door closed and carried me down to the first floor of the production studio.

We were hosting a large press conference that evening to make the announcement of who would be joining me on *Down Low* and then moving into a dinner and dance event for the crew. We were packing up and leaving for Rio the next week, and tonight was the night to try and gel a little as a team and have some fun doing it.

"Hey you." I looked up to see Nancy walking toward me. She took good care of making sure I looked the part no matter what she had going on. As my make-up artist, she'd seen me through some rough fucking mornings and helped me to disguise my pain through some less-than-stellar life choices.

"Hi, Nancy. You wanna come make me look pretty before this thing starts?" I gave her an award-winning smile and wrapped an arm around her frail shoulders. She could have been my grandmother and I would have been better off for it. At least I'd have some family besides my brother Liam.

"You bet, handsome." She glanced up at me as I pulled from her and opened the door, holding it to let her go through. "Your dark circles are getting worse. Are you using the cucumbers on your eyes?"

"Nope. I use them for other pleasures." I winked and offered her my arm.

"Dear God, please tell me that you just ate them."

"Something like that, yeah." I nodded toward my trailer. "We going in there for this rendezvous or do you need light?"

She chuckled. "Go get dressed and meet me in your dressing room. Your trailer has an odd vibe to it."

"Wait, what? Like what kind of vibe?" I crossed my arms over my chest and gave her a look my mother would be proud of if the old bitch paid any attention to me.

"Just a vibe." She shrugged. "Forget I said anything."

"Oh, hell no." I moved toward her and gripped her shoulders lightly. "Is it at least a good vibe?"

"Yeah, of course." She adverted her eyes.

"Liar. What's the vibe in there?" I glanced back and tilted my head, trying to think if she meant smell instead of vibe. It always seemed fresh and clean to me, but maybe she was one of those clean-freak people.

"It's dark and the place is bare, Ethan."

I turned and released her. "It's a temporary place to live while we're shooting."

"You've had that trailer for three years. It's not temporary." She reached up and brushed her fingers over the soft skin below my eyes. "Have you decorated your house yet?"

"No, but what does that have to do with the vibe in my trailer?" I snorted, not wanting to dive into whatever she was headed toward, and yet she wouldn't let me escape the truth.

"It has nothing to do with the trailer, and everything to do with you." She poked me in the chest and offered me a weak smile. "Get dressed in that black button down and grey slacks. Actually, put on the slacks and bring the shirt with you."

"You're trying to seduce me again, aren't you?" I winked and took a step back as she chuckled.

"We all are, love." She turned and left me there with the realization of what the vibe was.

Emptiness.

Chapter 2

Riley

"Excuse me! Excuse me! Waitress!" The older lady that stood, yelling at me from the back of the restaurant, had been giving me hell since the moment she sat down at my table.

I cleared my throat and apologized to the guy who was trying to order at one of my other tables.

"I'll be right back. Sorry about this." I gave him a sweet smile that I didn't feel and walked back toward her in time to watch her drop down into her chair with a loud huff. "I'm sorry, ma'am. What can I help you with?"

"Firstly, you can take this steak back to the kitchen. I said *medium rare* and this is not medium rare at all." She poked at the steak on her plate and glanced back up at me. "What did you write down? Medium well?"

"No, ma'am. I wrote down medium rare. I'm happy to-"

"Let me see your tablet." She extended her hand and watched me with complete disdain. It had been *that day* already, so having the wicked witch of the west seated in my section was no big surprise. The fact that I had exactly thirty minutes after my shift to drop off a late paper with my English professor and change for the Eon press conference that night had my stomach in knots. I'd been running back and forth to the bathroom my whole damn shift.

"Wilma. Jeez." The little old man beside her offered me a weak smile. "It's all right, dear. Just get the steak fixed."

"It's not all right. Let me see the tablet." She popped the table twice, causing me to jump. Where I wasn't at all docile, having someone snap at me when I was riding on E and headed toward a long night of hiding myself behind a facade of indifference was too much to handle.

I pulled my notepad from my front pocket and handed it to her as I picked up her plate and walked it back into the kitchen.

"This was supposed to be medium rare." I set it on the counter as the chef pulled it close and rolled his eyes.

"That *is* medium rare. See this?" He poked at it and blood oozed out onto the plate. "Learn your cooking temperatures, Riley. You're wasting my time."

"Great, well, the woman at my table is having a fucking conniption because it's not medium rare to her. Can you please throw another steak on the grill for her? Today's not the day for this." I put my hands on my hips, suddenly so damn tired of my old life.

Barely skimming by from paycheck to paycheck left me angry and quick to tear someone's throat out. The situation with my mother losing our house and lying about keeping my things safe in the process unraveled me even more. I had a bright future ahead of me for sure, but seeing that I was stuck in the present, the future was a world away.

"No. Take it back out there and tell her that the steak is medium rare. Period." He narrowed his eyes on me before turning around and going back to the insanity in the kitchen. The rumors at the restaurant that I'd seen Ethan Lewis had half the place loving me, and the other half not wanting anything to do with me. It was like I was 'selling out' by trying to make something better of my life. Fuck them too.

"Fine." I turned and walked back out to the table.

"Here. Obviously it's not you who's an idiot, unless you put in the wrong thing when you typed it in. Where is the ticket you submitted? I want to see it," the woman barked and handed me back my notepad.

The masculine voice behind me caused me to jump. "Hey, we're just going to grab something from somewhere else. This is taking forever."

"No, don't do that. I'll be right with you. I promise." Inadequacy raced through me, and I couldn't help but wonder for the hundredth time why I had decided to wait tables. Nothing was more stressful. People were rude, uncaring assholes on good days...

"I was talking to you first!" the woman barked and stood up.

"You know what? Get your own damn steak." I took off my apron, pulled my keys and what little bit of cash I had from it, and tossed it on the table. "I hope no one ruins your day like you've ruined mine."

I turned and walked out of the restaurant not feeling free like I wish I did, but worrying about how I was going to help Charlotte pay rent until my first advance from Eon Productions came in. I wished it was the worst of my worries, but it wasn't. Facing Ethan Lewis for the first time in almost a week was.

I'd lied about the almost kiss at his house a week before. Shameful pride left me trying to backtrack and cover up my need to push our budding relationship into something it never would be, nor should it. Even more than that, the sickening realization that he was seeing someone, or at least sleeping with her, was devastating. Why I thought an icon like him didn't have women warming his bed every other night of the week was beyond me. He wasn't living a normal man's life. He wasn't a boy I'd met at school at the coffee shop and our love affair would soon start.

He was Ethan fucking Lewis and *this* wasn't the movies. I needed to remember that above all else.

I got into my clunky car and tried to start the engine only to have the car sputter and die.

"No. Please. Come on. Not today. I just made up half an hour. Don't take it back from me," I growled and rubbed the dashboard as I tried again. "Come on, baby. Start up."

Nothing. The fucking thing wouldn't even turn over.

I let my head drop as someone tapped on my window. My manager, Gerald.

"Fucking awesome." I opened the door and got out of the car seeing that I didn't have the ability to roll the window down.

"Where are you going? Someone confronts you over a steak you mess up, and you quit? That doesn't sound like you at all. What's gotten into you? This isn't how the real world works. It's not a film." His words were far harsher than they should have been due to his tone and the ugly scowl on his face.

"I'm tired, Gerald. Taking one more person's shit today is likely to send me into being postal. I thought it would be best to walk out instead of try and explain to the woman who was ripping me a new one that her order was right. That I didn't mess up, the kitchen didn't mess up, no one fucking messed up. She wants someone to beat down, and honestly, I'm too beat down by my own shit right now to take anyone else's."

"That's stupid." He put his hands on his hips and narrowed his eyes. "Get back inside and apologize to her."

"I'd rather eat a turd." I leaned down into the car and got my wallet out of the console. "Thanks for the last few years. I quit."

"Don't ask me for a reference. Quitters don't get advances in life." He moved back as I pulled my phone from my purse and started toward home. It was five miles, but I was praying that I could get a hold of my best friend Charlotte, or if nothing else, my fuck-buddy Jace. Surely someone would be free.

"Okay. Thanks for that. It was only three years of my life of never missing a shift, getting here early and always smiling no matter how much my life or this shitty job sucked." I shook my head in disgust and pulled the phone to my ear as it rang. He continued to yap, but I walked down the street with my chin up, ignoring him.

How ready I was for a different life. I wasn't sure the life that Ethan lived was necessarily the one I was after, but one where I didn't have to search for change in the bottom of my car for gas or a loaf of bread at the store would be righteous. To have people pawing at me and worshiping the ground I walked on sounded horrid, but I would take that any day for a paycheck capable of pulling me out of poverty.

Charlotte's phone sent me to voice-mail, and I growled loudly and called Jace instead. He answered on the first ring.

"Hey, baby girl. What's up? Need me?" The laughter in the background told me quickly that he wasn't alone.

"I'm stuck on the side of the road off Vance and Timmons. Can you come give me a ride or are you too busy?" I kept my tone light. Jace was a good guy with a healthy lust for women – all women. He didn't deserve my shit, and after us being friends with benefits since our senior year in high school, he didn't much put up with it either.

"I'm good. Just leaving a barbecue. I'll be there in three minutes. I'm actually just down the road. Must be your lucky day." He chuckled.

"Not really, but thanks." I dropped the call and stopped on the side of the road to find somewhere to sit. It was still chilly out, but would be warming up soon. Spring in Los Angeles was fantastic and half the reason I still lived there. The other half was the hope that I'd eventually make it as an actress, and it would seem I had.

I still couldn't wrap my mind around the idea of being a part of a motion picture. One that people bought tickets to and gathered their friends to see. They would buy buckets of popcorn and a cold soda to sit down in a cold theater and see me. Well, see Ethan Lewis, but me too.

Ethan Lewis.

A long sigh left me as I brushed my fingers through my short strawberry-blond hair and tried not to ride that train of thought too long. Between his wavy chestnut hair and warm brown eyes, I was barely keeping my nose above the water. He had a million personalities that ranged from cheeky to sweet to insanely sexy to dominant. I wanted to know about each of them and get intimate with him in ways that would leave us both drowning.

But... I was being unreasonable. I was a nobody for now. That would change over time, but even that scared me to think about. And even as a nobody, I didn't look anything like the slutty blond he'd obviously taken to his bed after our meeting the week before, nor did I look like Trish Desmount. They were glamorous and I was plain.

"And filthy." I glanced down at my white shirt that was stained with food from my long shift at the restaurant.

"Hey, sexy. You need a ride?" Jace smiled and waved me over to his navy blue mustang. "I got a car and a cock with your name on it."

"You finally had my name tattooed on your jimmy?" I laughed as he scoffed.

"Come find out, Riley." It was a challenge I wouldn't make good on for a little while the way my calendar was stacking up, but as soon as I could... I would. Having him paw at me sounded delicious, fun, healing.

I gathering my stuff and realizing that my folder with my paper that was due was back in the employee locker room at the restaurant. "Fuck," I grumbled and walked to the car.

"What's up, buttercup?" He reached over and cupped the side of my face, pulling me in for a long kiss.

I melted into it as my eyes fluttered close. He was like coming home. How quickly I could see us turning into something more than we were, and where I wanted that a week back, I wasn't so sure anymore. Ethan seem to be working to take up more and more of my mental energy, and funny enough, he hadn't done a damn thing to deserve the space. He had actually done everything *not* to.

"I left my paper back at the restaurant." I kissed him again and moved back, licking at my lips and enjoying the subtle peppermint flavor of his tongue.

"Let's go get it." He watched me as if waiting for approval of his plan.

"No. Just take me home. I have that big-ass party for the film crew tonight. They're going to do a press conference and announce me as the female lead." I shrugged. My excitement was pressed below the weight of having to work with Ethan after I lied about my intent. Hurting him the way I had seemed wrong and took the joy out of a moment in my life that I should have been beyond elated about. Between that and being tired from not sleeping, I was sucking at life.

"You sure?" He gripped my hand and pulled it into his lap, stroking his erection with both our hands.

I chuckled and pulled my hand back. "I'm sure."

"I wanna go with you. Can you take a date?" He licked at the side of his mouth and gave me a sexy grin. "Might meet the woman of my dreams there."

"I thought *I* was the woman of your dreams." I snorted and pulled out my phone, texting Charlotte to see if she was still going with me too.

"You are baby, but you're taken." He reached over and ran his fingers up my thigh softly.

"No, I'm not." I trapped his hand. "Don't. I don't have time for anything other than getting ready. I want to look my best."

"You are taken." He pulled back and let out a soft sigh. "You belong to your career and the idea that I'll one day wake up a good guy."

I rolled my eyes and reached for the door handle as he pulled up to my apartment. "You can come tonight with me if you want to. Charlotte is coming too."

"Can I have you when we get back from it?" He reached over and brushed his fingers down my neck before gripping it softly. "Will you let me strip you down and bathe you with my tongue, fuck you with my fingers?"

Warmth danced in the center of my stomach, but cooled quickly at the simple fact that he wasn't Ethan. For some odd reason my libido was convinced that my soon-to-be co-star was the only man who could make me writhe in pleasure. I obviously needed a reset.

"Absolutely," I lied and leaned across the console of the car and kissed him hard and deep, letting my eyes close as he tugged me into his seat more. Our kiss turned into a quick petting session, and I was aching and dripping wet by the time I untangled from him and got out of the car.

At least I'd proven to myself that it wasn't just Ethan that could get me going, or was it? I couldn't deny that Jace had become him behind my closed eyes.

Chapter 3

Ethan

"Oh, you look much better." Deza stopped in front of me as I walked into the auditorium where the press was buzzing about in droves.

"So I looked like shit before?" I glanced around and groaned as several of them headed my way. "I fucking hate these things."

"Smile and be nice." She patted my chest like someone would a pet.

"And what's in it for me if I do?" I gave her a cheeky grin as she rolled her eyes and moved away from me.

"Mr. Lewis. Do you have time for a question?" The reporter shoved his microphone in my face and bumped it against my lips. "Sorry about that."

I hid my disdain and brushed my fingers over my mouth before smiling. "Of course. Make it quick though. I have no favorites and you're sure making it look like I do. Someone might run a story on me being in bed with your station if we're not careful."

The guy laughed. "No, really, I just wanted to ask how you guys decided to go with a nobody for this role. America is amazed at your generosity and such, but this girl..." he glanced down and fumbled with his notes, "Riley something-or-other... she's just a college kid with a hard life. Why-"

"Riley Phillips. She's a very talented actress," I barked, losing my cool. The little shit could suck a nut, as could the rest of the world. I might make a shit-ton of money and have the type of fame most people could only dream of, but to put Riley down and make her out to be nothing... nobody? Fuck that. "She came into the studio and stole our hearts. Not everyone gets recognized for their gifts or their talent. This profession is a game of luck most days of the week, but this time, it rolled in favor of a talented, beautiful woman."

"Oh, of course. One more-"

I put my hand on the mic and pushed back as she walked into the room from across the auditorium. Her cream-colored dress was dainty and made her look so much softer than I knew she was. My pulse spiked dramatically, and I couldn't help but move around the weasel in front of me and work to get closer to her warmth. Radiant was an understatement.

A good-looking guy a little taller than me moved up on her left and slipped his hand into hers as she glanced up and laughed at something he said.

"Shit. Who's that?" I stopped in my tracks and slipped my hands into my pockets. Was she dating him? She'd mentioned going out with someone when we first met, but through our brief interactions after that first encounter, I'd quickly deduced that she was single. It would seem that I was wrong.

"What are you looking at?" Deza stopped beside me and chuckled. "Oh, I see."

"Who's the jock with the shitty buzz cut?" I tilted my head to the side and let my eyes move down the soft curve of her breasts over her flat stomach to her long legs. The straps from her heels were wound up her leg to mid-calf. I wanted so badly to hit the floor and work them off of her sensually, slowly as she laid back and let me have her for the night.

"No clue." She tugged at my sleeve. "Stop staring at her like you're a starving man who's finally found his first meal."

"Not his first, but the buffet he wants to bury his face in." I licked at my lips and moved toward her as Deza slipped her arm into mine.

"Please don't be a dick tonight. I'm begging."

"I love it when you beg." I glanced down at her and winked. "If you'd do it on your knees more often I might actually come anywhere you wanted me to."

"You're gross."

"It was your dirty mind that took my comment there." I laughed low in my chest, grateful for something to chuckle about as we approached Riley and her beau. "I was just being compliant with your wishes."

"Riley. We're going to get started soon, so let's get you to the back and touch up your make-up for the cameras." Deza moved in front of me and blocked my view of her for a minute.

I extended my hand to her rent-a-date. "I'm Ethan. Nice to meet you, man. You are?"

"Hey. Great films. I've seen most of them." He smiled and I could see why she liked him. He had a bad boy appeal. I hated him already. "I'm Jace Dillon."

"That name could score you a few films of your own." I shook his hand and slipped my hands back in my pockets. Nervous habit.

"Hi Ethan!" Riley's pretty blond friend moved around Jace and stopped in front of me.

"Hey Jade. How are you?" I extended my hand only to have her move in for a tight hug.

Riley smiled as I glanced over at her. "You'll have to get used to this. She's part of the deal when you guys signed me."

"I don't mind." I gave the girl a quick hug, but didn't take my eyes off my beautiful co-star. "Tell Deza to suck a dick. You don't need any help with your make-up. You look stunning already."

She rolled her eyes and moved toward me, surprising me a little as she reached up, cupped my cheek and brushed her thumb just under my eye.

"You're wearing some. I should too." She moved back with a sweet smile on her face.

"I have to. The demons won't let me sleep at night." I winked and turned to Deza as she snorted.

"Stop calling women demons. It's demeaning." She turned and beckoned Riley to join her. I wanted to as well, but it seemed silly.

There was almost a flood of relief inside of me that Riley seemed back to being her old self. Having her upset with me, or tense in my presence in a way that wasn't cheeky, was unnerving, and we'd just met. I liked our relationship the way it was. If she were willing to get over the small mishaps we had the week before, I could too. I'd even let the idea of her *testing* me go. It was a far better answer than thinking I had hurt her pride. Hell had no fury like a woman scorned. Even *they* would agree with that.

"So you have a way with the ladies as well?" Jace asked and crossed his arms over his chest. I hated how quickly I was to judge him, but the poor guy didn't stand a chance with me. He was standing too close to the woman I wanted wrapped around me later that night. He had something I wanted - badly, and I wasn't too used to that.

"Naw... I give them what they want from time to time and go about my merry way." I shrugged and pointed toward the drink table. "Jade, there're bottles of water over there. You want to grab a few for us?"

"It's Charlotte, but sure." She smiled and walked with a pep in her step toward the beverage table. I wasn't trying to be a male chauvinist pig, but I needed some time alone with Bubba on my left to see what he thought he had going on with Riley.

"I like that. You'll have to tell me how to get women to serve you so easily." The tall asshole chuckled.

"It's not too hard." I rolled my shoulders. "Riley doesn't serve you, I guess?"

He laughed loudly. "Riley? Fuck no. That girl wears the pants in her world. She's far too dominant to let a man tell her what to do. The *only* time she relents is in the bedroom."

White-hot anger burned down the center of my chest, and I lost the ability to suck air into my lungs for a few seconds.

"Here you go!" Charlotte, or Jade, or whoever Riley's friend was, extended a bottle of water to me and then to Jace.

He shook his head and patted my back. "Nice to meet you, Ethan. I'm getting a beer before this shindig starts."

"You too, man." I took the water and glanced down at the girl as she stared at me with stars in her eyes. "You look pretty tonight."

"I do? Really?" She smiled and turned from me as a soft squeal left her. My stalker-dar lit up with a bright warning to run like hell.

"Yep. Tell me more about Riley and Jace. Are they a couple? She didn't mention being with anyone, but it's totally cool if she is." I shrugged as she glanced back over at me.

"It's complicated. You know?" She moved closer. "Are you dating someone?"

"Nope. It's in my contract that I have to remain single. Sucks, but it's the way they do things." I lifted my finger as she started to ask another question. "If you'll excuse me. We'll catch up later. I think they're getting started."

"Oh, sure. Of course." She moved out of my way, which was a relief I hadn't expected to experience. Most girls like her wouldn't let me go too quickly, at least not without pawing at me or getting in a few awkward selfies.

"Let's get this part over with." Frank patted my back as he moved up next to me and walked with me up to the stage.

"Agreed. I hate this shit," I mumbled and scanned the crowd. "Where are the girls?"

"The adoring fans?" He gave me a warning look.

"No, my future baby-momma and my pimp, Riley and Deza." I glanced back toward the restrooms to see her and Deza walking out.

"Please don't do anything we're all going to regret later." He patted my back again and took his seat.

I pulled out two of the chairs at the long table before me and waited until they got on the stage to offer a kind smile. I wasn't going to regret a damn thing other than never experiencing the beautiful creature who had effectively fucked up my world.

"Ladies..." I winked and pushed up their chairs before taking mine between Riley and Frank.

She glanced over at me and smiled. "I like the black shirt. It accentuates your masculinity, Mr. Lewis."

I leaned over and pressed my lips to her ear and the cameras flashed all around us as I chuckled. Her compliment was odd and I wasn't sure if it was a compliment at all. "You didn't need that make-up. You looked incredible the minute you walked in. The whole fucking room took notice."

She turned and caught me off guard with her nearness. "I'm glad they did, but what about you?"

"Did you want me to?" I let my eyes move down to the swell of her ruby-red lips.

"Not a chance," she whispered as another picture was taken. She turned back to the front and rested her forearms on the table. "We should get this party started."

The crowd of reporters laughed and clapped.

She was worried about the world noticing her, and I was almost scared to let them. It wouldn't take long, and she'd be dancing along the clouds with the rest of us stars in LA. Little did she know that I'd be waiting in the wings when the dust settled and the illusion wore off. She'd need protecting, and I'd made her a promise I intended to keep - no matter what.

"Are you just completely thrilled to be working next to 'the Ethan Lewis' like, the one and only?" One of the energetic reporters from NBC stood before me and Riley after the press conference portion of the night was over. Security was working to get all of them out the door so the rest of us could let our hair down and try to enjoy the party set up for us, but it was like shooing roaches. One disappeared to have two show up in its place.

Riley glanced over at me and gave me a tight smile. "He's so much more than you guys could ever imagine."

"I'm not just half an ass. I'm a complete ass." I winked at the reporter and put my arm around Riley's lower back, leading her toward the drink table "All right, superstar 101 is to never let them see the real you. Fake them out as best you can and keep them guessing."

"Who is they?" She pressed her hands to the bar in front of us and arched her back as she stretched. The soft groan that left her had my balls tightening. They could be whoever she wanted them to be. Hell, I could be whoever she wanted me to be as well. At least for a night. I was too selfish for much more than that.

"Exactly, right? I hate they, but in our example, they is the news media, the reporters and your fans." I brushed my fingers over the small of her back and nibbled at my bottom lip as she subtly moved away. "Your family, co-actors and close friends are usually a good bet, but anyone else? Hell no. Be on guard."

She turned and studied my face as if looking for something. An invitation maybe? Fuck, I wished. I'd jump right on that.

"Do you only have Frank, Deza and your brother?" She licked at her lips subtly. The mere glimpse of her pretty pink tongue had my cock rising to attention in hopes of being petted by her.

"How do you know about my brother?" I smiled and tried to rein in my need to move in without worrying about her desires to remain professional. I was only a man. She couldn't expect too much from me, and if she did, she might find herself highly disappointed. I swallowed hard as my thoughts took a turn for the worse.

Can you take a dick, sweet girl? Can you not only play the game, but bring home the win?

"Charlotte mentioned him."

"Charlotte, as in Jade?" I chuckled and brushed my fingers over my lips as I forced myself not to glance down the front of her dress to take in the beauty of her cleavage. She wasn't too big up front, and I was glad. I wanted a handful to hold, a mouthful to suck, but nothing more.

"Yeah, that's her." She glanced around as if looking for her. "Did you get to meet Jace?"

"I did. Is he your boyfriend that you mentioned a week back?" My insides tightened at the thought of her dating someone. I wasn't beyond being a home-wrecker by any means, but I was hoping her answer might leave me with some margin to be normal while stealing her heart.

Her heart? No. That was far too high up for my goals. I wanted between her thighs. Nothing more.

"No one is willing to start the buffet line. You guys get up there and eat, please. Let's get this shit started so we can go home and get in our pjs soon. " Deza stopped beside us, interrupting our intimate conversation and leaving me without an answer.

"We're having a pj party tonight? I sleep nude." I shrugged as Riley chuckled and Deza growled.

"I'm not shy, and to be completely honest, I'm starving." Riley turned and walked to the long buffet line where her man stood, not looking nearly as pissy as I would have been about her standing close to another man. Did they have one of those odd relationships where they let other members into their bed? Like swingers or something close to it? *Odd.*

"What the fuck was that?" I turned to my agent and put my hands on my hips. "I almost had her seduced. You owe me."

"You did not. Stop acting like a dick and eat." She pushed softly at my chest.

"You stop acting and eat a dick. I have one you can practice with." I laughed as she pushed at me.

"I swear you're ten years old most days."

"More like fifteen, but close." I put my arm over her shoulders and squeezed. "Find out who Jace is and help me get rid of him."

"Nope. That's not happening." She pulled from me.

"All right. Then game on." I popped her ass hard and walked to the table, picking up the platter of shrimp and walking toward the door. "Fuck you guys. I'm going to hang out with the only big kahuna-"

"Shit, Ethan. Fine. Ugh. Put the shrimp back and behave," she growled at me. "I hate you sometimes."

"No, you don't. You wish you did, but you just can't do it, can you?" I winked and set the shrimp down before looking back at a group of staff with a cocky smile on my face. "Just dicking around with my wife. She likes it when I do that... anything with my dick really."

Laughter filled the room as she smacked me and growled at them, "Don't encourage his lies."

Chapter 4

Riley

I rolled my eyes at Ethan's antics. He was too cute for his own good, but the sad part was that he was more than aware of it, and taken.

"I'm going to have his children. I've decided." Charlotte let out a girlie sigh next to me.

Jace picked up a plate. "I don't see what the hype is all about. He seems like a regular dude with a little bit of make-up and a fruity-ass haircut."

My need to defend Ethan roared to life, but I pushed it back down. He didn't need to be defended, and I'd never seen Jace get upset or jealous over another guy. It was almost humorous.

"Don't be a hater," I mumbled and pressed my shoulder against his as we moved down the buffet.

"Why would I be hating on him? He just has everything in the world that any man could possibly want, and then some. The fucker has the perfect life." Jace rolled his shoulders and sighed.

"Well, he doesn't have me." I was only teasing, but the look on Jace's face said that he didn't have me either. Not that I was the end all be all. I wasn't. Not for either of them obviously.

"That looks good." Ethan moved in on the other side of Charlotte and plucked a cherry tomato off her plate.

She giggled as I lifted my eyebrow at him. "You're in rare form tonight."

He bounced on his feet and shrugged. "I'm excited. I love the start of a new filming session. It feels like my slate's been wiped clean and it's time to start over."

"Your slate being wiped clean?" I turned my attention back to the table. "That would be one hell of a job for the one with the Windex."

"You're telling me. My arm hurts just thinking about it." He reached for the same piece of cheese I was working to get and plucked it from the tray. "I'm guessing you have nothing on your slate that needs to be removed, Miss Goodie-Goodie?"

"When are we leaving for Rio?" I ignored his comments as my lip tugged up into a smile. I liked him teasing me in any way that he would, but letting him know it was out. He was already convinced that he was a Casanova to a hurting world. I wasn't adding to that shit in the slightest. I busied myself with filling my plate as Charlotte stumbled over herself and Jace moved stiffly beside me. Awkward wouldn't begin to cover it.

"I think Tuesday or Wednesday next week. I can't keep up with the schedule. That's why we have *schedulers*." He moved around Charlotte and squeezed in between us. "I go when they say go, and I come when they say come."

"Sounds like they have a tight grip on your balls." I glanced up at him and lifted my eyebrow. I wanted a tight grip on his balls, but getting one was going to prove to be challenging and perhaps more effort than it was worth. Ethan probably changed women the way most people changed underwear.

"Mmmmm... just like I like it." He lifted a tomato toward my lips and smiled. "I do believe I owe you a testing period."

"What? That makes no sense." I leaned in and took the tomato without thinking too much about it. Jace cleared his throat behind me and slid an arm around the back of my waist.

"A testing period over what?" he asked, his voice low and husky.

Ethan ignored him, seeming almost comfortable in the midst of what could turn out to be something quite ugly.

"Yeah. You tested me and I passed. I think I should return the favor." He lifted a tomato to his lips and sucked it into his mouth.

I hated how badly he affected me. Warmth spread down my stomach and swirled between my thighs, leaving me far more needy than the man before me would ever know about. I wanted a kiss. Just one. The memory of the hard press of his lips against mine during my first audition was lost to how nervous I was trying to keep it together and score the part.

"And why in the world would you plan to test me, Mr. Lewis?" I took a step closer as Jace released me, growled softly and walked with Charlotte to a nearby table.

"You could be after my assets as much as a woman who simply pretends to be a fan. I think if I tease you mercilessly and you don't give in to my advances that we can safely say that you're just simply a great actress with no agenda." He winked and walked around me, brushing his shoulder against my back ever so softly before stopping on the other side of me at the table.

"You'll have to get close enough to tease me." I moved by him as he stopped to pick up a napkin. "Good luck with that one."

"Rehearsal starts on Tuesday, I believe." He licked his lips and winked at me. "Best of luck getting through that unscathed."

"You wouldn't do that." I walked with him to the table where Jace and Charlotte were, and sat down, half-expecting him to find another table. When he sat down across from us, I glanced up in shock.

"Of course I would. I made sure not to give you too much trouble during the audition because they were watching you so closely, but now... game on, right?" He seemed to be ignoring the fact that we had other people at our table, Jace especially.

What an ass. What if Jace was my boyfriend? Ethan didn't know the truth of our relationship, and regardless of that, Jace was my date. For Ethan to be so crass around him told me one thing... he was a spoiled brat that expected to get what he wanted no matter who might get hurt. Some of the lust I had dancing inside of me dimmed.

"So I quit my job today." I glanced over at Charlotte, changing the subject.

"And her car broke down." Jace wrapped an arm over my shoulder. "Long day for the prettiest girl in LA."

I gave him a cheeky grin and couldn't help but notice how Ethan's gaze darkened. Was he jealous? Surely not, though the thought caused my heart to beat faster. It was silly and childish as hell. I needed to teach him a lesson or two on how to be a better human in general, but the girlie part of me was thrilled with the possibility that the Hollywood icon of our generation wanted my attention. Me. A nobody.

"We need to get you a new car. You have to have reliable transportation to get places on time." Ethan had no emotion in his words. He was pissed or tired of being around us from what I could gather.

Jace pulled out his phone and grumbled, "I need to take this."

"I'll go out with you. I forgot my phone in the car." Charlotte got up and followed my handsome date outside.

"How long have you guys been together?" Ethan's voice softened a little, but the disapproval on his face was obvious as he poked his fork around on his plate.

"I've known Jace for a little over five years now." I took a bite of the chicken on my plate. "He's a good guy. Captain of the rugby team at UCLA where I go to school."

"Awesome." He glanced down at his plate. "You know it's hard to maintain a relationship when we have to travel so much. Not to mention how jealous guys get when their girls are making out with someone else on screen."

He glanced up as I sat back in my chair. Our relationship was going to be a fucking roller coaster at best. I could only pray that our highs were going to be good enough to sustain the drop offs.

"I remember you telling me that." I smiled. "Right before you reworded my question to make it less about you and more about actors in general."

"It's hard to let someone in, Riley. I'm sure as we get to know each other more and work together for an extended period of time, you'll come to know more of me than you ever wanted to." He pushed his food around the plate, but kept his gaze locked on to mine. I was beyond intimidated and yet there was no way I was breaking the stare. Something hot as hell sat between us. Maybe it was fame that birthed lust between two co-stars. I'd seen too many stories of actors leaving their wives for their co-stars. I was starting to see why. Separating fantasy from reality was going to be a challenge.

"What if I want to know everything?" I licked at the tip of my fork as his eyes lifted.

"I have a biography you can read." He winked and glanced around as Deza approached and sat down beside him.

"Hey, kids. Congratulations to you both. Frank and I are thrilled to have things going this well." She reached for the salt in the middle of the table.

Darren's voice surprised me as he spoke just behind me. I hadn't let him go as my agent yet, so I wasn't sure why I was so taken aback by him being there, but I was.

"I'm proud of you too." Darren rubbed my back and sat down to my left. "I'm so sorry about not calling you with Eon's offer. I honestly had so much shit go down with my momma-"

Deza lifted her head as her eyes widened a little. "What's wrong with your momma?"

"She had a heart attack. It's been a long-ass week." He ran his fingers down his face. "I should go. I don't deserve to be here."

"No, it's okay." I reached back and took his hand. "It all worked out."

"Not because of me." He shook his head and couldn't seem to keep his eyes off Deza. Something beautiful existed below the surface of the odd relationship between them. I'd have to find out more later from him or her... or both of them. Why weren't they together when it was more than obvious that they should be?

"Let's go talk. You want to?" Deza moved back from the table and walked around, offering Darren her hand. "Just me and you?"

"I'd love that." His voice was soft, endearing.

I turned to watch them go as tears filled my eyes.

"Wow. That's the first time I've ever seen Deza give up eating for anything." Ethan chuckled as I reached for my napkin and turned back to face him. "Hey. What's wrong?"

"Nothing. I just hope things work out for them." I blotted my eyes and glanced up to the ceiling. "Acting is my passion, but can you imagine if life really included feeling some of the things we fake?"

"I wish," he mumbled and gave me a soft smile. "To be completely honest, I can almost feel those emotions when I act. If I have the right co-star."

"I think you pull off those emotions beautifully if you have the right co-star or not." I took another bite of my dinner and studied him as he returned the favor. "You have the heart of America sitting in the palm of your hand. It must be exhilarating and frightening all in the same moment."

"It's exhausting, but I make it work. I've been doing it too long to know anything different." He picked up his plate and moved to sit in the seat right next to me, scoring me with his nearness.

The scent of his cologne filled my senses and left me weak. "Do you think you'll always be an actor?"

"Of course. What else would I be? The expectation has been set, and I'm rather stuck dancing along to the tune the puppeteer plays." He shrugged. "This is the life for me. Only love could pull me from it, but I already told you that it's harder than you think to find love after you've made it big. It's a good thing you have Jace, and that you really *know* him. That will give you a bit of comfort when shit gets rough, because it will."

The look on his handsome face told me that he was hiding behind a mask. He was depressed, moody, but why? Was he like that often and I was just getting to see behind the curtain a little?

"You want to dance now that the dance floor is filling up?" I brushed my napkin across my lips and moved to stand.

"You just want to get your hands on me. Naughty girl." He got up and gripped my hand tightly as he moved us to the center of the floor.

"I'm failing your first test miserably, aren't I?" I slid my hands up his thick chest and felt the need to apologize again for lying about the kiss. If the memory of seeing the hot blond at his door that same night hadn't kicked me in the face and filled me with regret, I would have. Fuck him for denying me and then taking another woman to his bed.

"I failed yours." He smiled and rested his hands on my lower back.

Some part of me wanted him to inch his fingers lower until he grasped me intimately as I had him in our second try-out scene. The soft feel of his flesh beneath my fingers wouldn't be something I would soon forget.

"No, you passed mine, remember." I looked up into his warm brown eyes and saw something that scared me. Neediness. Was he lonely? Was I willing to do anything about it? Could I and survive?

Tell him. Tell him that it wasn't a test. Tell him that you came back to express how much you wanted to stay the night, to get lost in his arms. Tell him!

"No, I don't think I did." He breathed in deeply and spun me to the left, pushing me from him only to pull me back closely. "You know there is a dancing scene in this next movie, right?"

"Really? I haven't seen the script. When will I get it?"

"When we get on the plane next week." His fingertips brushed along the top curve of my ass, causing my heart to race harder. "You're panting, Riley. Why?"

"What is the scene?" I ignored him as I was getting good at doing.

He awarded me with a cheeky smile. "It's a tango scene in a restaurant. Do you tango?" He licked his lips and moved closer. The strong press of his erection against my stomach left my insides melting. I'd never been with a man his size, much less seen someone sporting so much dick. The thought of getting my hands on him and seeing what I could do was incredibly exhilarating.

Warmth raced up my chest and coated my neck and cheeks as my nipples budded tightly. I wrapped my arms around his neck and brushed the tiny pebbles against him, wanting him to know that whatever he was thinking... I was thinking it too.

"I can learn." I spun and pressed my back against his chest as his hand slid over my stomach and locked me tightly to him.

"Somehow I believe that." His lips grazed past my ear. "Your boyfriend might not like how close we're dancing."

"True. Let's not upset him, lest he take his anger out on my body later tonight." I pulled from him and walked back toward our table as Jace and Charlotte entered the room again. No reason to make Jace jealous, not that I thought it was possible, but to cause Ethan's blood to burn?

Now that was my *deepest* desire.

Chapter 5

Ethan

Bitch. Man she was such a bitch. A bitch I wanted groaning my name and begging for more of what only I could give her.

"Dude, really?" Deza moved to stand in front of me as she wiped at her eyes. She'd been crying.

"What?" I reached out and brushed my hands over her shoulders before looking behind her for Darren. I was going to whoop his ass if he hurt her. "Where is he?"

"No. We're good." She rested her hands on my chest. "His mom had a heart attack and isn't doing too well."

"What were you getting onto me for?" I turned my attention back to her, grateful that she was okay. I didn't have many people in my life that I'd defend, but Deza was one of them. Something told me that Riley was soon to join the crew.

"Your dick is halfway up your stomach. Are you seriously thinking that no one is going to notice that?"

I glanced down and released her before tugging my shirt out of my pants and rolled my shoulders. "Better?"

"Yeah." She patted my chest and glanced over her shoulder. "What is it about this girl?"

"No clue." I moved past Deza as Trish walked into the room. "I plan to find out though."

Riley was being a cheeky bitch by teasing me with her bedroom talk about Jace, but two could play her game. I wasn't going to stand on the side of the dance floor like a junior high boy with my dick caught in my zipper. Nope. Not happening. Besides, the pretty little tart still believed that Trish was my wettest dream. No reason not to exploit that.

"Hey, beautiful." I stopped in front of Trish as she paused by Riley's table and gave me a warm smile. I was happy as hell not to see her new hubby on her arm. She most likely got an invite just for being one of Deza's clients.

"Hi, Ethan." She slipped her hands into mine and leaned in for a kiss. "This looks fun."

"It's the same old shit if you wanna be honest about it." I turned her and wrapped an arm around her lower back as my eyes met Riley's. "Hey, guys. I'd love for you to meet Trish Desmount. She's a co-star of mine and my childhood crush."

I forced warmth up to coat my cheeks by thinking of an embarrassing moment from my childhood. It had nothing to do with anything, but by the look on Riley's pretty face, she was falling for my shit, hook, line and sinker. My brother, Liam, would be proud.

"Oh, stop it." Trish glanced over at me and blushed herself. "Everyone knows that you're the big stuff in Hollywood."

"Maybe, but you're right beside me." I let my eyes move across her pretty face and allowed an uncomfortable silence to fall between all of us. It was almost too easy.

"Right, well, I'm Riley. This is my friend, Charlotte and my man, Jace." Riley stood up and walked around the table toward us.

"Oh, yeah. Nice to meet you Riley." Trish leaned across the front of me.

I kept my eyes on her and breathed in softly, just loudly enough for Riley to hear. The laughter that bubbled up inside of me was locked behind my clenched jaw.

"The pleasure is all mine." Riley shook Trish's hand as her friends stood and did the same.

I finally released the pretty blond and moved back, but kept my attention on just her. The weight of Riley's eyes on me left my stomach tightening, my pulse quickening.

"I'm thirsty." Trish glanced back at me as Deza walked up and handed me a phone.

"You left this on the table. Liam's on it." Deza pulled Trish into a quick hug after I took the phone and turned to walk toward the windows.

"What's up, bro?" It took everything inside of me not to look over my shoulder to see if my girl was watching me. *She's not your girl, idiot.*

"Hey, man. You still with me this weekend?" Liam's voice was professional. He was still in the office.

"Yeah. We're going out on the boat on Saturday?" I turned and tried to find Riley with my peripheral vision, failing miserably and turning around fully. She and Jace were on the dance floor, looking more and more like the couple I would grow to hate.

"Yep. You need a bitch, or you got one?" He cleared his throat.

I rolled my eyes. Where I'd have been more than happy to think of women as objects a few years back, Deza was finally influencing me for the better.

"I'll find someone to come with me. Those girls you pick are all the same." I crossed my free arm across my chest and let my eyes run down the back of Riley's dress to the swell of her ass. "I have the perfect girl for the trip, but she's unfortunately taken."

"This the same one you were whimpering about last week?" He chuckled.

"Yep. Fuck you too. I gotta go. I'll see you at the dock at ten on Saturday. You good with Deza and Frank joining us?"

"Yep, and make it nine."

"Suck a nut." I hung up the phone and slipped it into my pocket as I walked back toward the dance floor. It was a dick move to cut in, but I was totally doing it.

Trish moved in front of me and put her hand on my chest, stopping me. "Hey."

"Hey, Trish." My expression softened as I let my guard down a little. Of all the people I'd worked with over the years, Trish was my favorite. She was like the sister I never had and might actually like. Deza was like the one that would put ants in your bed and shave your eyebrows when you slept.

"You okay? You were being really weird earlier." She lifted her eyebrows and pursed her lips.

"Oh. Right." I glanced down and gave her a sheepish smile. "I really wanted to make Riley jealous, so I kinda told her that you were my crush."

"Your crush?" She laughed and touched the side of my face. "That's so damn cute."

"All right. Stop it." I cupped my hand over hers and searched her face. She wasn't teasing me in a malicious way from what I could tell. "It didn't work as you'll see." I nodded toward the dance floor. "Her Channing Tatum-looking boyfriend is spinning her around the dance floor a little too well."

"Hmmm." Trish turned and moved to stand beside me as I slipped my hands into my pockets.

"I got a hard-on during our audition the other day."

"No. Really?" She glanced over at me with surprise on her face.

"I know, right? First time since I was a kid with too much gusto." I wagged my eyebrows and turned back to watch Riley. "There's something about her."

"You know that you need to be careful. Falling for a co-worker is death to an actor's career." She pressed her head against my arm and chuckled softly. "And just so you know, they aren't together."

"Who isn't together?" I turned my face toward her and thought about kissing her forehead just in case Riley was watching, but decided against it. I might be a class-A asshole, but having anyone believe that Trish was cheating on her new man was out.

"Riley and her date." She moved away from me and seemed to be studying them. "I've watched lots of romance films in my life. You know, trying to get better. I swear I can do just about anything but fake lust."

"Yep. You do suck at faking the sexy stuff." I laughed as she yelped and popped me in the stomach playfully.

"You turd." She turned back toward the floor. "I shouldn't help you for that."

"Please? Pretty please with a big juicy cherry on top? A cherry I'd like to-"

"All right. Jeez." She laughed nervously. "See the way he grips her hips as they dance close? He wants control of her but doesn't have it."

"What? How do you know that?"

She turned to face me. "If you and I weren't lovers, but you wanted us to be. How would you hold me while we were dancing?"

I glanced out at the dance floor and then back to her as I turned to face her. "I guess I'd grip your hips to remind you who should be in control. Seems like the natural way to act. But I'd do that if we were together too."

"No you wouldn't." She shook her head.

I chuckled. "Yeah. I would."

"Nope." She slid her hands up my chest and moved closer. "Play with me for a minute."

"I thought you'd never ask." I reached out and gripped her hips tightly.

"No, you buffoon. Really. Close your eyes and imagine me to be the one woman that lights up your nights with more passion than you ever deserved. We aren't just lovers, we're in love. You belong to me and me to you." She reached up and brushed her fingers over my eyes. "Close your eyes and imagine it."

I closed my eyes and gave her a cocky smirk as I sucked in a quick breath of air and sank down into character. She was Riley within seconds though I barely knew the poor girl. I'd been with a million women over the last ten years and yet no one had stained my desire the way she had. I yearned to simply take her to bed for one night to see if she was everything I'd built her up to be. I'd most likely be disappointed as I was every time I took my clothes off, but the possibility was there of finding something different, something overwhelming and right.

"Now... Reach out and hold me like we're dancing in the kitchen. It's just me and you, Ethan, and I'm her, whoever she is." Trish slipped her hand up over my chest and grasped her hands together just behind my neck.

I kept my eyes closed and ran my hands down her extended arms, over her sides and down to cup her ass tightly. I leaned down and pressed my face to the crook of her neck and breathed in deeply.

"Yeah. They aren't together." I moved back and turned to the floor as Trish took a shaky breath and moved away from me.

"Remind me not to play match maker again." She fanned herself and walked toward the drink table. "You're too much for even me."

"That's right, girl. Don't forget it either." I moved to the edge of the floor and watched them for a few more minutes. My mind wanted to fold and agree to the fact that she was taken, but too much of it didn't add up. There was heat between her and Jace, but it was a familiarity, a comfortable heat. Something like Deza and I might experience if we ever let ourselves start fucking. Maybe that was it. Maybe they were just fuck buddies.

"You look lonely." Riley smiled as she walked toward the edge of the floor. Jace was headed toward the bar, which gave me the only chance I might get that night.

"Me? Never. All the voices in my head keep me company." I offered her a hand. "Dance with me again?"

"Sure." She slipped her hand into mine and moved out onto the floor before turning to face me. "So how is it that you're in love with Trish and she's married?"

"It sucks, right? Nothing ever really is fair in love and war." I gripped her wrists and tugged her closer before lifting her arms and clasping her hands around my neck for her. "She's taken and I just have to get over it."

"I would say that you already have." She glanced down, but moved in closer, pressing her sexy little body against mine and starting my show and tell below my belt all over again. The sadness that brushed across her face caused me to pause in the middle of the dance floor.

"What are you talking about? I'm not here with anyone. How have I moved on?" I forced myself to stop making up shit in my head and start asking. I'd have a million lies spun around Riley and her actions before we left for the night if I wasn't careful.

"The blond that slept over last week." She glanced up at me as her expression tightened. She was closing down on me.

I softly ran my hands over her hips and gripped them tightly. I couldn't seem to force myself to finish the deal. To slide them over her ass and pull her in closer, to speak a million words without having to open my mouth.

"I don't know what blond you're referring to." I swallowed hard. Her nearness had desire swelling in my stomach and pressing a hot ball of need up my chest. Every part of me wanted to experience her. Why, though? She was stunning no doubt, but it wasn't just her looks. I'd held a million beautiful women in my arms over the years. It was her denial of me, her authenticity to remain unmoved by my shit. I loved it.

"Never mind." She licked at her lips and turned to smile at someone.

I glanced over to see Jace watching her like a hawk.

"Hey. My brother is taking me, Deza and Frank out for a trip to Catalina Island for the day. I'd like for you to come with us, unless you're busy." I wanted to grip her chin and force her to look back at me, but it would give away too much.

"Saturday?" She turned her attention back to me. "Yeah, let me just ask Jace what we have going on."

I smiled. "Yeah. Do that for me."

She was lying, and I almost loved the effort she was putting into making me jealous. The asshole in me wanted to tell her just how *cute* it was, but I let it go. Not letting her on to just how jealous I was would be a much better bet.

Chapter 6

Two Days Later
Riley

"Are you sure I can't go with you?" Charlotte gave me the saddest look I'd ever seen on her face.

"No, but next time I'll make sure they let me bring a friend, okay? Today we're going over stuff for the movie. You know they can't have anyone else hear that but those of us who signed our lives away to them." I turned around in the bathroom, making sure the white cotton dress I had over my shorts and bikini top looked the part. Casual, but elegant.

"Isn't Ethan's brother going? He's not signed his life away." She flopped back on my bed and let out a long groan. "Besides. I want to meet him. He's so funny in Ethan's bio."

"I guess I need to read this damn biography." I ran my fingers through my short hair before grabbing a tube of hooker-red lipstick and putting a little one. I needed more color in my face, and Nancy wasn't exactly available to help a sister out. Funny how quickly I'd come to want the attention that my future was going to provide.

"Did you hear me? Liam didn't sign a confidentiality agreement." She sat up and huffed again.

"You don't know that, and I'm the new kid on the block, Char. Ethan has them wrapped around his fingers. He's Ethan Lewis. Hell, he has the world wrapped around his fingers." I rolled my eyes at the thought and let my mind move back to the party the week before.

I'd forced myself to ask about the blond who spent the night at his house after our pseudo-meeting, but he seemed confused. Maybe I should have mentioned that he was moaning like a whore in the early morning light of the weekend. Maybe not. It really wasn't any of my business. I wanted to know who she was, but the truth would only send me scurrying toward dark emotions that wouldn't help either of us.

He could live his life, and I'd live mine.

"Make sure you take sunscreen." Charlotte got up and walked out of my room. "I have some in the kitchen, in the cabinet above the stove."

"In the kitchen?" I slipped my feet into my sandals and grabbed my bag. "You know that stuff doesn't keep you from getting burnt while you're cooking, right?"

I laughed at the look she gave me. She was upset about not going with me on the day trip to Catalina Island with Ethan and the crew, but it wasn't within my control to take her.

"You're dumb." She pulled the bottle from the cabinet and tossed it to me. "Have you heard from your mom? Did you tell her about signing the papers for the movie?"

"No. I need to try and call her before we leave for filming in Rio. Her phone wasn't picking up last night when I tried, which of course can't mean anything good." I let out a long sigh and tried to stifle the need to cancel my plans and go in search of her. She was a grown woman and yet was still making decisions like she was a wayward teenager. Without much to live for, she seemed to be searching out situations and people that could pull her from the edge of apathy toward truly living. Somehow it felt like she was on the road to self-destruct, much like my brother Derick had been.

"I'll be here if she needs something." Charlotte pulled me into a hug. "Have fun, okay, and don't break Ethan's heart."

"What? Don't be silly. He's got his heart locked into a tiny box somewhere in that big, strong chest of his." I rolled my eyes as I pulled back. "I can assure you that he's quite safe."

"You think that, but he's just flesh and blood, Riley." She squeezed my shoulders and walked languidly back toward the bedroom. "Have fun and don't do anything that I wouldn't do."

That left the door open for a whole host of fun things to try...

"Ethan, you didn't tell me she was stunning." A handsome guy with dark brown hair and warm brown eyes reached for my hand as I walked up to the yacht where some familiar looking people stood around talking.

"Yes, I believe I did, and if I didn't, there was a reason for it." Ethan moved up beside me and put his arm over my shoulders. "Riley Phillips, meet my devious older brother, Liam Lewis. He's a scoundrel and a half, so watch him very closely."

Liam shook my hand and rolled his eyes. "Don't listen to a word he says. He's just worried I'll steal his girl, his house and his job."

"All in the same damn day, no doubt." Ethan released me and walked toward the boat. "Let's go peeps. Time to get this show on the road, or water as it were."

"Nice to meet you." I gave Liam a shy smile and pulled the strap to my bag up farther on my shoulder as Deza moved in closer and gave me a warm smile.

"The pleasure is all mine, pretty lady." Liam winked and jogged to catch up with Ethan.

"Wow. He's hot." I glanced over at Deza.

"And a total asshole. Keep that in mind." She crossed her arms over her chest.

"It might run in the family." I laughed and took the hand that Frank offered as we moved up onto the platform that led to the boat.

"Morning, Riley. You look pretty today." He gave me a warm, fatherly smile.

"Morning. You do too." I chuckled and moved past him, unable to keep my eyes from moving down and checking out Ethan's ass in his shorts. He had to be the sexiest man I'd ever laid eyes on. I wanted to see under the layers of clothing, and yet to do so would only muddy the already tainted waters between us.

He hopped down into the boat beside his brother and turned, lifting his hands to offer me help.

"I got it, but thank you." I moved to the side and hopped down beside him. "I love the water. Thanks for the invite."

"Of course. We were going to discuss a few scenes from the film, so you had to be here." He winked and offered Deza help too. She took it and thanked him before kicking off her sandals and pulling off her top. Ethan whistled playfully at her, and I couldn't help but enjoy their relationship. If he and I didn't turn out to be lovers, I had to hope we could at least be really great friends like they were.

"Look but don't touch." She wagged her finger at him.

"Damn. I thought I was your type." His lip turned down into a frown.

"Not even close, Mister. Your skin is far too light for my liking." She shrugged and turned to walk toward the edge of the boat.

"I can get it dyed. I'm sure Nancy has something that would help us out. No need to let our love only go skin deep, Deza." He glanced over at me as his lip rose in a sexy smirk. "You like black men too, Riley?"

"Who doesn't?" I dropped my bag and purse on the boat beside me and kicked off my sandals. "They have incredible packages they usually bring to the relationship."

"Amen to that, sister." Deza glanced over her shoulder and laughed loudly as Ethan's expression changed with his emotion.

"I have a great package, thank you very much." He put his hands on his hips as Frank laughed and walked to join us at the edge of the boat.

"You need one for someone to put up with your personality." He patted Ethan on the back and moved to the other side of me as we laughed.

"You guys love me, and hate that it's keeping you up at night. I know jealousy when I see it." The sound of his voice rolled over me as I pressed my forearms to the railing and let my eyes move across the turbulent sea. It was beautiful and breathtaking, much like the handsome man behind me.

"All right beautiful people." I turned as Liam stopped beside Ethan and smiled. "Just a few rules on the boat today. No jumping off the side while we're moving, and no pushing Ethan off either. He's my retirement plan and if you harm him, I'll be forced to work until I'm at least forty. That's not happening, so behave."

We laughed as Ethan rolled his eyes and glanced over to his brother. To say Liam was handsome would have been an understatement. He was as good looking as his little brother and seemed to have a great personality, much like Ethan did as well. I wanted to know more about him seeing that he was the *only* person in Ethan's life from what Charlotte had told me.

"He's all of our retirement plans. No one is hurting the goods," Frank added his two cents.

"Keep it up, and I'll make sure to act a fucking fool in Rio." Ethan shrugged and gave us an adorable grin like only he could.

"Something tells me that you're going to do that no matter what we do." Deza moved over to him and pulled him into a hug from the side. "You've yet to grow up."

"Grow up? Who said anything about growing up?" His eyes moved over my face as he smiled. "Riley can be the grown up on the crew. She'll help you guys keep me in line."

"We don't have the funding to pay her to put up with you." Deza squeezed him as he groaned loudly. "I say we throw him overboard. Who's with me?"

I laughed and turned my back to them, enjoying the comradery, but feeling a little like I was on the outside looking in. It would take some time to get used to working with a close-knit group, but I'd get it down eventually.

"So Ethan tells me that you're a film student at UCLA." Liam moved up beside me and leaned against the railing, but left a comfortable distance between us.

"I am. I should graduate in May if I can work with my professors to help me out during these trips we're taking. They're all pretty excited for me, but rules are still rules." I smiled at him. "What do you do for a living?"

"I own an advertising agency that caters to women." He clasped his hands together and turned a little more toward me. "We have more female CEOs in Cali than anywhere else in the world. It just made sense to set up shop after college and cater to them, you know?"

"Brilliant targeted marketing. I love it." I glanced back out at the water. "And you never wanted to be an actor like Ethan is?"

"Hell no." He chuckled. "No offense, but having people pretend to love you in the business world is hard enough. I can't imagine having to do that shit on the big screen. Everyone thinks they know you, but they don't."

"Right." I glanced back to see Deza, Frank and Ethan laughing about something. The happiness on Ethan's face as he interacted with the other two members of our intimate-sized team warmed me. There was so much more to him than he was giving me access to. Maybe time would help forge a bond between us.

"He thinks you're quite special." Liam slipped his hands into his pockets. "I'd say he just might be right."

"Oh yeah?" I stood up and tilted my head to the side, studying Ethan's older brother closely. "And how would you know? You've just met me. It would seem that you, Mr. Lewis, are as much of a playboy as your younger brother."

"She's figuring us out, Liam. I told you she was beautiful *and* dangerous." Ethan moved up beside me as he tugged his polo over his head.

"Stop showing off." Liam popped him in the stomach and walked back toward the center of the boat.

"I'm not showing off. I just want some sun on my chest." He licked at the side of his mouth and turned his gaze onto me. "Was that showing off?"

"I don't think so, but maybe your brother knows something we don't." I laughed and reached down, pulling my dress off and tossing it toward the pile of stuff that belonged to me. I glanced down and fixed my bikini top to make sure I had full coverage.

Chapter 7

Ethan

Damn.

I wasn't sure she could be any more fine than she was. The small white triangles that covered her nipples left plenty of creamy flesh on display for everyone to ogle over. The protective side of me wanted to bark at her to put her dress back on, while the alpha in me wanted to demand that she take off her shorts too. I wanted to see the bottoms almost more than I wanted my next breath.

"Like what you see?" She gave me a cocky smile.

"Yep. I sure do." I licked at my lips again and glanced up to see Liam talking with Deza. "My brother was supposed to bring a girl with him today. I'm wondering if she canceled or he did."

I followed his line of sight. "Is he dating someone?"

"He's dating everyone. He's a whore, but I love him for it." I ran my hands down my chest and took the opportunity to sneak another look at her. "He's the big shit in his world, but somehow he balances his life a little better than I balance mine."

"How so?" She turned her big blue eyes my way, and my heart fluttered in my chest. It was almost comical.

"He goes with the flow, and is honestly upbeat most of the time. I haven't seen Liam down or depressed more than three times in our lives, and each of them were in moments of great loss where you would expect to see it."

"So you guys are close?" She ran her fingers over the strap of her bathing suit as she glanced down and tugged at the fabric.

"Yeah, he's my best friend outside of D." I reached out and pulled her hand down. "You look amazing. Stop dicking with that."

"Thanks." She dropped her hands to the side and let out a sigh. "I just want to make sure I don't look too slutty."

"Too slutty? You need to stop worrying what anyone else thinks before we get into a situation where every-fucking-body has an opinion. Just dress like you wanna dress, live like you wanna live and Deza will chew your ass for the rest."

Deza walked up beside us. "I thought I heard my name."

"You did. I was talking about the best sex I've ever had." I wagged my eyebrows only to catch a backhand in the stomach.

"Get real." She rolled her eyes. "Riley, come up here and let's look at a few parts of the contract you signed and then we'll gather up and go over the overall plot for the movie and look at some of the first scenes that we'll be shooting next week."

My pretty co-star nodded and walked off with Deza as Frank joined me.

"You happy with our ultimate choice?" He leaned against the railing of the boat and crossed his arms over his large chest.

"Very. She's incredibly talented and beautiful to boot." I brushed my fingers by my lips. "Now if I could just figure out how to get her to do a lap dance for me."

"No, no and no." He laughed and sat down on the bench beside him. "She's going to hopefully be able to stay with us through the next three films. Having her early in her career leaves me to believe that we'll get to hold on to her for a little while before other producers come knocking on her door."

"She needs a new agent. Darren isn't doing anything for her career." I couldn't seem to pull my eyes off of her. She stood near the front of the boat, talking with Deza and laughing, and I was almost jealous. I wanted more of her time.

"This is true. Make sure you tell her that. Breaking off the relationship she has with Darren is key in moving her career forward. I think Deza spoke with her about coming over to the dark side and letting Deza represent her, but in all the madness, I guess it hasn't happened just yet." Frank shrugged as I turned my attention back to him.

"Is it weird that I want her career to go farther than mine has?" I hated the way my heart fluttered at the sight of her, but maybe I was moving beyond my own self-centered need to feel wanted.

Liam moved up to stand in front of me and gave me *that* smile. "Is it weird that for the first time in our lives, I want to steal the girl of your dreams from you and make her moan?"

"Fuck you, nugget head." I popped him in the chest.

"She's hands off for both of you." Frank stood up and stretched. "No tainting the pretty thing to think all men are the dicks that you two are."

"That hurts me, Frank." I grabbed my chest. "That hurts me real bad."

He laughed and walked over toward Deza and Riley.

"Man... she's so fucking hot, Ethan. I'd love to take her below the deck and undo that top with my teeth. I bet she's tight as hell too. Virgin? You think she's a-"

I popped him again. "Shut it up, dude. Seriously. You're not getting in her panties. I am."

"Naw, come on, man. That wouldn't work out well for you. You know sleeping with anyone at work is the worst possible thing you could do. You guys have a great night of passion, and then you realize you conquered the chase and it's over. She still wants more, namely because you've got a firehose in your pants, and you're ready to move on. What then? I'll tell you what then... ten months of having to deal with her emotions and your misery. I love you too much to put you through that. Let me just have her."

I laughed at his stupid antics. "I thought you just told me the other day that you were hiring some dominant chick that you were going to use up and toss to the road. Is she not a co-worker?"

"No. That's different." He shrugged and turned to watch Riley again. I had to push down the need to throw his ass off the moving boat, thus breaking the rules and my mother's tainted heart. "This chick at work knows what she's coming into *and* she's not my co-worker. I'm her boss. I'm going to school her ass on how to properly suck a dick. That's our first lesson."

I laughed loudly. "Don't go near Riley or I'm liable to break your face."

"Really?" He turned back and pinned me with an inquisitive stare. "You really like this chick enough to get your ass handed to you by your older brother?"

"Yep." I slipped my hands into my pockets and glanced up to find her watching me. "I'm not sure if *like* is the right word, but I want her to myself, whether it happens or not. You're not getting near her."

"Aww... man. You know how good her moans would sound coming up out of the bedroom down there?" He laughed as I turned and moved toward him aggressively. He lifted his hands and laughed. "All right. All right. I was just kidding. I'll lay off, shit. Obviously this girl has magical powers. Just promise me you'll kiss and tell. Just with her. I just gotta know."

"Go make yourself useful and fall off the front of the boat so the motor will chop your ass up and bring in those pretty great whites that I love to see." I turned to face the water and was almost glad to hear him walking off. The sound of his sardonic laughter would normally have me chuckling too, but for some reason I couldn't muster it.

Liam might be a total cock, but his idea of taking Riley below deck and making her moan was a delicious one. I let my mind dance along the possibility.

"Get on the bed." I nodded toward it as she watched me with a need that burned the inside of my soul and left me wanting to bend over and pant like I'd run a hundred miles.

"How do you want me?" She reached up and undid the strap around her neck, letting the top fall down as she worked on the string around her back. Her perky breasts were enticing, her nipples budded and a dark pink. My mouth watered at the sight of her being so innocent, when I knew she wasn't.

"On your back, baby." I slipped my shorts over my hips and watched her eyes widen a little. She'd seen a little bit of me through various wardrobe mishaps and perhaps in the lining of my shorts when I got aroused around her from time to time, but never naked. Never fully erect and ready to take advantage of the passion that lay between us.

"Beautiful." She moved toward me and reached out, stroking me once as she pressed her chest to mine. The warmth of her sun-kissed skin was enough to melt me.

I groaned and slid my hand up her back to her head as I pulled her in for a long, probing kiss. She gripped my side with one of her hands and continued to stroke me with the other. Every muscle in my body was locked into place as heat danced along my pleasure points, licking, teasing, begging me to come.

"Hey. You look lonely down here." Riley's voice pulled me from my daydream.

"Hey." I sucked in a deep breath and stood up. "Damn. I got lost in my thoughts."

She gave me a look that said she could tell.

I glanced down and grumbled as I readjusted myself and looked for my shirt. "I swear. The curse of being well-endowed. God forbid I have a sensual thought and my body reacts to it. Everyone in the fucking universe will know."

She bent over and handed me the shirt. "I don't think you should worry about it. It's just us."

"Yeah, but D will give me hell, and if she fails too, my brother will be standing in line just behind her with pom poms." I laughed and pulled the shirt over my head. I should have been more embarrassed, but Riley's presence was a comfort in ways that didn't make sense.

"What were you thinking about?" Her cheeks colored pink, and I couldn't help but laugh. She was innocent and sweet in appearance when she wanted to be, and a sexy minx at other times. She had as many masks as I did, and hers probably came with a new hairdo to boot.

"How nice it would be to bake in the sun, and then slip below deck and make love to a beautiful woman for the afternoon." I lifted my arms toward the light blue sky and let out a yawn as I stretched.

"And would you cast Trish or the blond from your house the other day?" The light in her eyes dimmed a little. I still couldn't figure out what blond she was talking about.

"What?" I tugged my shirt down again. "What blond do you keep referring to?"

"The other night when we had dinner at your house and you refused my kiss." She gave me a cheeky smile and turned toward the water.

"I was being tested, remember?" I turned and pressed my shoulder against hers as I breathed in deeply, hoping to take the scent of her down deep into my lungs.

"Who was she?" She glanced over at me as the wind blew hard. It was the perfect moment to slide my fingers into her hair and pull her against me for a long, dramatic kiss. I almost lamented over the fact that I was stuck in a movie in my head, one that wouldn't let me come up for air.

"It was just me and you that night, remember? We didn't even drink that much. Have you lost your mind to fantasy already?" I reached out and brushed her hair from her face as my pulse spiked.

She swatted me away as her facade cracked a little. "After I left. She came to the door and said that you were busy for the rest of the evening. She had long blond hair, loads of make-up."

Jazz. Fuck. Was Riley the one at the door that night? I knew I'd heard someone beating on the front door as I lost myself to orgasm over and over. Fuck. Surely not.

"Did you come back after you left?" Sickness pulsed through me. I didn't much care that people thought me to be a playboy, but to have Riley think I was a whore was out. I would never get into her bed with her thinking that I took loads of loose women to mine, which I did.

"You're circling the question and not answering me. Why?"

"Because it's none of your business." I smiled and tapped the tip of her perfect nose before turning my attention back to the water. I was being an ass with my answer, but in all reality, it was true. It wasn't any of her business.

Chapter 8

Riley

His answer stung me in a way that left me wanting to find a bathroom and let out a few tears. I glanced back toward the water and swallowed the hot ball of anger in my throat. Why had I even asked? It wasn't my business. I'd already made that determination, and to follow through with asking him about the girl only left me looking like a love-sick idiot, which I wasn't.

"That's very true." I shrugged and let out a soft sigh as if I was totally taken by the beauty of the ocean. "Whoever she was, she was beautiful."

He snorted and shook his head. "This life isn't easy. It's not like I can have a real relationship. All I have is a few warm bodies to keep offering me false hope that there is more to love than a quick fuck."

Now he was cracking. Some nefarious part of me wanted to clap and release a maniacal laugh. I wanted down into his heart. Wanted to know who the real Ethan Lewis was. It would take time to find him through the layers of lies and false character roles he'd taken on over his short life, but I had hope that eventually I would stand face to face with a man that no one had seen before. The real him.

"Are you saying that I should find a few bodies to keep me warm too?" I didn't look his way, I couldn't.

"You have Jace, remember?" He pressed his forearms to the railing and turned to stare at me.

"But when we're gone for months at a time." I glanced over at him, which was a complete mistake. The desire in his eyes was palpable. He knew how to get what he wanted, and if I planned to survive for any extended period around him, my best bet would be to deflect or to make sure that I wasn't at all what he thought he wanted. Something told me that neither plan was necessarily good enough to leave me free from yearning for his attention or his affection.

"You're willing to cheat on your boyfriend?" His words had an almost laugh accompanying them. "He wouldn't mind having someone work you into a sweaty mess?"

"We have an open relationship." I shrugged as if it were no big deal. It was a partial truth at least.

"Interesting." He pressed his shoulder to mine. "No sleeping with anyone in a foreign country, and honestly, you need to be careful in general. Have you lived anywhere besides Los Angeles?"

"No. I grew up there and have always lived within a three-mile radius of where I am now." I sounded as naive as I felt all of a sudden.

"Right, well, let me tell you from intimate experience that the world is happy to offer you love, lust and a good fucking time until the morning sun comes up. Then you're on your own to deal with the consequences of your momentary *needs*." He rolled his eyes and grimaced. "I'm lucky that nothing has happened thus far, but I'm sure my turn is coming."

"Why chance it? Just find someone from your childhood that you know and feel safe with and have a friends with benefits-type set up." I hated to push him in that direction, but the emotion on his face left me with little choice. Offer myself up, which wasn't happening, or help him find something more reasonable for his lonely nights. This was me, of course, assuming that blondie with the big tits wasn't an old friend.

"I don't have friends from childhood, Riley. I've lived this life the whole time, remember?" He pressed his shoulder to mine again. "It's all good. I have a few girls I can call on, but we're not talking about me... we're talking about you, this is assuming that you're the kind of girl who wants or needs sex on a regular basis to keep sane."

We were getting a little too intimate for my liking. There was no way in hell that I was telling him that I was the kind of woman that would prefer sex at least once a day if it was available, and that was a minimum. Half of my depression or fucked up mood swings lately had come from me and Jace becoming less and less regular. To have months between sessions meant that my punch card at the *Love Shack* was getting used more often than not. I'd been through three vibrators in the last six months, and more batteries than I cared to consider.

"So the blond was just one of your girls?" I smiled as he growled softly beside me.

"Yes. Jazz is one of my girls. You're horrible at deflecting, though you try to use that card all the damn time." He shook his head as his eyes moved across my face. "Do you like a lot of sex in your life, or just a little here and there?"

"That's none of your business." I lifted my eyebrow, throwing him back the same sinking life vest that he offered me moments before.

"Sure it is." He stood up and I turned to face him. "I was going to offer myself up in your times of need, but if you're looking for three times a day, I figured I might have to start charging you."

Heat swelled deep inside my belly. Ethan Lewis was offering himself up to be my personal sex slave? Surely not.

"And what exactly would you charge for an all-nighter, Mr. Lewis?" I lifted my fist toward his face as if I had a mic. "Your adoring fans want to know."

"Hmm..." he glanced around and gave me a contemplative look, as if he were deep in thought. "I think it would be based on services rendered. For oral sex, we'll go with a hundred thousand dollars."

My nipples tightened to the point of aching. "And are we talking about giving or receiving?"

"Oh, giving. I love pussy." He licked at his lips, toying with me. How we'd jumped this deep into the pool was beyond me, but I wasn't willing to relent or let him know for a second just how insanely turned on I was.

"Of course, and what about them giving oral sex? Would that be a charge too, or-"

"Heavens yes." He gave me a cute look. "However, I would be willing to give a deep discount if the girl could properly give a blow job."

"Properly... hmm, that's interesting. Do you have a handbook that I could pass out, by chance?" I fanned myself and let my eyelashes flutter as if he were getting to me.

He laughed deep in his chest, stealing my heart with the sound. He might not know anything about me, and I might only know the surface of who he really was, but after watching him grow up on screen for the last ten years, I loved various parts of who I thought him to be. We all did. It was impossible not to.

"A handbook. Now *that* is a great idea."

I pulled down my hand as Liam joined us. The warmth that spread up my chest and coated my cheeks was all too real this time. Where I could be playful and have a bit of fun with Ethan, it felt trite to do it with anyone else, at least to the extreme we were taking it.

"A handbook for what?" Liam moved to my side and leaned against the railing behind me.

"For cock sucking. Riley thinks that my fans might like to have an instructional manual on how to please me. She might be on to something here." Ethan wagged his eyebrows, obviously very comfortable in front of his brother.

"Oh, I like that. Would we have pictures and how-tos?" Liam winked at me. "You know it might be hard to get that monster to fit on the page. We could shrink it down and just have a caption off to the side that says, 'not actual size'."

I laughed and snorted before pressing my hand to my face. "You guys are horrible."

"Yes, we love depravity as much as the next guy." Liam shrugged.

"Or girl." Ethan pointed to me. "She might be able to give us a run for our money."

"We have lots of it between the two of us." Liam chuckled softly.

Deza walked up and put her hands on her hips. "What are you three plotting over here?"

"World domination," Liam offered up. "You want in?"

"Actually, the best way to suck a dick." Ethan gave an innocent look and shrugged.

"World domination through cock sucking." I couldn't help it, and the look I got from all three of them was well worth the comment leaving my lips.

"Oh, hell no." Deza grabbed my hand and pulled me away from them. "The last thing we need is for these two to influence you. No more talking to them together."

"It was Ethan." I glanced over my shoulder as he flipped me off with a sexy smile on his lips. "Make the manual. We can sell it next to the popcorn at our next movie."

"I like the sound of that," he called after me.

"What? The manual?" I pulled from Deza and turned to face him. I almost lamented over him having put his shirt back on, but no matter what he was wearing or wasn't, he was still a heartthrob through and through.

"Well, that, yes, but the thought of the next movie being ours." He winked at me and turned as Liam started to give him hell over being sentimental.

I let out a soft sigh and dropped down beside Frank as Ethan's offer raced through my mind. Had he offered to be my fuck-buddy while we were traveling? Surely not.

Yes, the hell he did.

"Uh oh." Frank reached out and patted my knee. "You got that look in your eyes that scares most men with any sense in their heads."

I laughed. "And what look would that be?"

"It's manipulation 101. You're trying to figure out how to get what you want and make the other guy or gal involved think it was their idea. I know how you smart girls work." He lifted his eyebrow, giving me a knowing look.

"Wow. You're good." I glanced up at Deza. "What're the rules on dating or sleeping with your co-workers on the set?"

"You and Ethan are *not* getting together. Hands off. Completely."

I lifted my hands. "I'm not interested in Ethan, but I didn't see anything about me dating the cameraman or one of the extras. People find themselves in precarious situations all the time. I want to be prepared. What're the rules, or are there any?"

"Just be smart about your decisions." Frank leaned back and closed his eyes as he clasped his hands over his belly. "Our jobs are hard enough as it were. You being pissy at someone on set during filming because of a break up or some other drama would just make it worse. And Deza is right. As much as you and Ethan seem to be hitting it off, it needs to be a solid working friendship and nothing more. No love or lust. It would fuck up everything, and you just got started."

"Good to know." I glanced down toward him to find him watching me closely.

Conflicting emotions tore up my insides, but I knew myself well enough to know that if nothing else happened, Ethan and I would most certainly be sharing a long sweaty night together, and it would be soon if I had any say in it.

Chapter 9

Ethan

"I should be rich enough at this point to have someone else pack for me. You do it. You dress me better than I dress myself anyway." I tossed a t-shirt at Deza and dropped down on my bed in nothing but a pair of boxer briefs.

"Cover that up. God." She walked into the room after bitching at me for ten minutes from the living room to hurry up. As if we had any-fucking-where to be that night. We didn't, and I was pretty sure the plane wasn't leaving without me.

"Don't be jealous. Get over it and I'll let you pet it too." I laughed deep in my chest as she tossed the t-shirt back at me and pretended to gag. "Keep it up. I know I'm close to breaking you down."

"Breaking me down." She turned and put her fist on her hip. "And what pray-tell does that mean?"

I sat up and licked my lips. "You tell me what the hell pray-tell means and I'll give in to your harassments. You can have an hour with me, okay?"

"I live my life with you, and you're too young to know what pray-tell means." She turned back to the closet and grumbled softly under her breath.

I moved to my stomach and wiggled my way to the edge of the bed, putting my chin in my hands and waiting for the opportunity to strike again. She worked through my clothes, pulling out various things and draping them over her arm.

"I don't get paid enough for this shit." She glanced back and lifted her eyebrow at me. "Are you checking me out?"

"Duh. Your ass looks good in those jeans. You're way too little for a big boy like me, but I can appreciate the ass for sure."

"I hate you sometimes." She turned back around as I rolled onto my back and scooted up a little more, letting my head hang off the bed.

"No you don't. You say it too much. People that really hate each other *show* it, and you only show me love." I smiled as she walked up beside me and dropped the clothes on the bed next to me. "No one else would put up with me... but you do, and it's because you love me."

"This is true." She sat down beside me and brushed my hair back, digging into my scalp with her fingers. Chill bumps covered my skin as I moved over and rested my head on her thigh. "I think I'm still in love with Darren. It's been ten years, and all I've thought about was him."

"Really?" I lifted my eyes to check her expression. I couldn't really tell if she were kidding or serious. She'd never mentioned Darren to me. To think that we had a close relationship and I didn't know that her ex-hubby had stolen her heart was pathetic. Maybe the relationship was one-sided, as in her taking care of me and me doing nothing in return.

"Really." She popped my forehead softly and got up. "Come on. We're going to be late. I know your King-I-Shit, but it's rude to waste other people's time."

"Agreed." I got up and pulled a pair of jeans over my legs as she stopped by the doorway and turned to watch me.

"Do you think I should give him another try?"

"If you think what you're feeling is love, then yes. I don't think it comes around very often. Seeing that you've not been with anyone since we've been together as a team, I'd say that you need to figure out if it's because of him or not." I pulled a shirt over my head and tucked it in. "What? Why the funny look?"

"Because you never cease to amaze me. You're so unbelievably dickish most days of the week, and yet there is a side to you that I don't believe anyone gets to see."

"It's the side where the sun don't shine." I turned and twerked.

The sound of her laughing as she walked down the hall warmed me. For the first time in my life, I wanted to protect her, to find out who Darren was and make sure he was on the up and up before D gave her heart to the bastard again only to have him give it back.

"Weird." I walked to the bathroom to brush my teeth. My eyes moved across my face, and for the first time in a long time, I didn't look like a zombie. I wasn't sleeping too well at night, but the rest of the time was spent thinking about Riley or making love to myself. Something about it was working for me.

I moved back and reached down into my jeans to readjust myself, hoping to make my shit look less obvious. I turned to the side and shook my head and tried again. Nope.

"What are you doing?" She glanced into the bathroom and lifted her eyebrow at me.

"Trying to make my dick lay down. You wanna help?"

"Why are we always on this subject?" She walked in and glanced down. "It looks fine. What are you worried about?"

"It's taking center stage. Look how badly it pokes out."

"No one would believe this crazy shit, not even if I videoed it." She walked out of the bathroom. "Get your stuff put in your suitcase and let's go. I'm leaving in three minutes. With or without you."

"Lies," I muttered and pressed my hand to the front of my pants as I walked back in the room, as if I had the ability to force the fucker to lay down. What was a blessing to most was a huge curse to me. Somehow being around Riley and having the bastard grow to its full potential should have horrified me, and yet it felt comfortable, right. Maybe it was because she promised to protect me, and had done a pretty damn good job of it so far. And we were only getting started.

I grabbed my stuff and walked to the front door as Deza opened it and walked out.

"You were serious? You were going to leave me?" I closed the door, locked it and muscled my bag out to the curb where the limo waited.

"Yep. I told you I was." She greeted the driver as I got into the back of the car and sunk down into the plush leather.

"Did you guys rent out a villa in Rio? You know I hate the thought of staying in a hotel where people can paw at me every time I leave my damn room." I tried to stifle the concern that Deza wouldn't have taken care of all of it. I'd never known her not to be at the top of her game where I was concerned.

"Of course we took care of it. We're in a seven-bedroom condo on the water. The scenes we're shooting over the next week and a half are all within a three-mile radius. We got a chef, a few maids and some other miscellaneous help. No one should bother you unless the bar you choose to go to has other tourists there. That's all on you."

"Not happening." I ran my fingers through my hair and contemplated talking to Deza about Riley. I knew how strict she'd been thus far about me and my pretty co-star not getting too cozy, but my proposition to Riley for us to be fuck-buddies was different. It was a safe way to live a little and yet not have to hide the evidence of simply being young, dumb and human.

"What are you thinking about? I can see your mind spinning over there." She crossed her arms across her chest. "It looks like you're plotting out something that I'd not be too thrilled to hear."

"Really? You can't give me the benefit of the doubt? I was thinking about what kind of flowers to buy you for your birthday next week."

"Bullshit. Spill. What's up?"

"Nothing." I pulled out my phone and ran through a few apps like I had anyone I wanted to talk to. I rarely showed up on social media because it was overwhelming. Besides, Deza had some poor schmuck who got paid to be me online. That was a fucked up job.

"I'm going to put you in the back of the plane by yourself if you don't tell me what's up." She reached over and squeezed my knee tightly.

I yelped and swatted her hand away. "I'm going to put you over my knee and pop that sexy ass of yours a few times if you don't watch it. I'm not ten anymore, and you're not in charge."

"Yes, I am." Her expression tightened as her bottom lip protruded.

"Don't do that." I rolled my eyes as she sunk down into her seat, pouting. "Come on, D. You know I can't deny you when you get all pouty. It's so cute it hurts."

"Tell me then." She turned in her seat and stared at me, still looking pouty.

"I can see why Darren likes you so much. He's missing out. That bottom lip would feel so good gliding over-"

"Never mind!" She pushed at my shoulder as I laughed. "I don't want to know that bad. Shit."

"You're not going to like what I have to say, and you're going to shut it down before I can get it out of my mouth, so no. I'm not telling you a damn thing about my thoughts this morning. My life is the same old shit all the time. I figured out a way to liven it up a little," I paused as she groaned loudly and pressed her palms to her eyes, "and keep myself safe doing it."

"You don't know the meaning of safe." She sat up. "Remember last summer when we were filming in the Bahamas and you went on that hang-gliding tour without checking into the company at all?"

"That was a fucking blast. You're just salty that you didn't come with me."

"No. I'm still pissed that you almost died, Ethan. This isn't just about your career. It's about your life."

"Which, by the way... sucks." I straightened my shoulders, not willing to back down. "Money and fame buy you one thing. You wanna know what it is?"

"Happiness?" She gave me a sheepish grin.

"Right. Try again. Loneliness."

"You're choosing that life because you refuse to trust anyone's intentions, Ethan. Not every woman is after your money or your man-beast." She glanced down at my lap. "Some of them might actually love you."

I snorted. "That's rich. They can't love me, Deza. They don't know me. They've watched me wear a million masks. Why am I the only one that gets this? Right, because it's my life."

"Tell me what you're thinking about doing, and I'll support it if I can."

"You don't. I promise." I moved toward the door as we pulled up to the hangar bay where the plane sat ready for us to take off.

"I will try. Just tell me. Trust me." She gripped my arm and softened me with the look on her face. She cared about me without a doubt, but part of that care was her overprotective side that drove me batty. I was a grown-ass man. I didn't need someone taping bubble-wrap around me every goddamn morning. It was getting old, and so was I - alone.

I got out of the car and walked to the back to pull out my luggage. The driver looked a little surprised when I refused his help and lugged the large suitcase out on my own.

"Ethan. Please?" She took her bag from me and walked on my left as we approached the plane. "Please."

"Fine." I turned to face her as we stood at the bottom of the stairs. The plane opened the door for us, and I lowered my voice just in case. "Riley and I were talking about how hard it is to travel and not have companionship. It's one thing to sleep with someone you know and take your chances, but to do it with a stranger in another country or some crazed-ass fan... it's just getting old, D. Okay?"

"What did you guys decide would work best?" Her face visibly paled.

I laughed. "Nope. See that right there. That look says that you're going to shut me down."

"Did you decide to be fuck buddies?" She gripped my arm and jerked me toward her. "That's not happening."

"We didn't decide anything. I offered and she failed to respond."

"Good for her. You know as well as I do that lust is a precursor to love."

"No, I don't know that story at all. Lust has been nothing but lust for me. Just another warm body to try and fuck only to end up miserable and alone." I pulled from her angrily. I shouldn't have said anything.

"I'm sorry you're going through some shit, Ethan, but this is a no go. It's not happening. Period."

I glanced up to find Riley standing in the doorway in a pair of short white shorts and a pink tank top. She looked good enough to eat.

"Morning. You guys okay?" She leaned over to look down at Deza. "What's a no go?"

"Nothing. Morning, beautiful." I moved past her into the plane and left her to talk with D. She could let the pretty bombshell know that my offer was void, not that she'd taken me up on it in the first place.

I wasn't that lucky...

Chapter 10

Riley

"What was that all about?" I moved back as Deza walked into the plane, looking less than thrilled to be there.

"Same old shit." She paused and seemed to force the smile that moved across her face. "How are you? Everything go okay with getting away for a few weeks? Your professors weren't assholes about it?"

"Most of them were good to me." I reached over and grabbed her bag as she tried to take it from me. I laughed and walked back to the small, but open space where a handful of leather chairs sat. "Morning, Ethan."

I lifted Deza's bag as he turned and took it from me. "How are you? Ready for us to get this show on the road? Nervous at all?"

"I'm excited. I've been waiting my whole life for something like this, but on a smaller scale." I moved back and dropped down in the seat closest to me.

"You're just going to have to jump from commercials to the big time. It's going to be an adjustment, but you'll love it." Deza sat down on my left and let out a sigh. "We'll be here to help you through it all."

"I'm going to call Frank to see what's taking the old goat so long," Ethan butted in and turned, walking to the front of the plane with a stiffness in his stride that didn't belong there. I prayed like hell that he wasn't pissy. A few wrong comments from him, and I'd be crawling in the pit with him.

Having to try and pinch pennies that morning with Charlotte to pay rent only to come up short had me wanting to lay down in the middle of a busy road.

"I appreciate your support. I think it's time I had a long talk with Darren though. I haven't released him yet, but it's probably better that I do if I'm going to be getting paid soon. He gets a cut of that, and he's honestly not done shit to deserve it." I reached down and buckled my seatbelt as my eyes moved up to covet Ethan's strong back and sexy rear as he hovered near the front of the plane.

The pilot walked out and they shook hands before he had Ethan sign something for his daughter.

"Let's just keep him on the payroll for now. I'll work as your agent, but we'll let him have the benefit of being listed as such. He's going through a hard time." Deza ran her fingers through her long hair. "I shouldn't help him out, but I'm not sure I have a choice."

"Why is that? You still love him?" I pulled my legs into the seat with me and shifted a little to give her my full attention.

"Yeah, I think I do." She shrugged and laid her head on her shoulder. "He's all I knew as a young girl, trying to make something out of myself. He helped me a lot in the beginning and loved me through some really tough stuff. I feel like I almost owe him something back in return."

"What happened to you guys?" It was none of my business and yet I couldn't help but dig a little. I wanted to help bring them back together if it meant both Darren and Deza could find love. It was a fleeting emotion for me, but like anyone with a beating heart, I wanted love to win somewhere in my world. Even if it wasn't directly connected to me.

"We were kids when we got married, and he honestly pulled me up out of a bad situation. I'd gotten into drugs and sleeping around, and his younger brother was my boyfriend at the time. Awkward, I know." She smiled.

"Wow. And was he into that stuff back then too?" I glanced up as the guys huddled at the front. Frank was standing near the cockpit with them, which was a good sign. I had to assume everyone else on the crew was taking a different flight, or was already out there, which wouldn't have surprised me much. There was a ton of work that went into setting up the scenes before we ever stepped foot on the sand.

"No, he graduated with his degree in criminal justice. He was going to be a cop." She let out a shaky sigh as her eyes filled with tears. "I'm sorry. So many good memories."

"No, it's okay." I reached out and ran my hand over her arm, squeezing softly. "I love getting to know more about you guys."

"I just wish I'd made some different decisions back then. Once he got me cleaned up, we both found out that we had a love for drama. We would go to plays all the time, and one thing kept emerging that forged our future."

"What was that?" I released her, but leaned in a little.

"The actors in those small independent films were sometimes so much better than the ones in the A-list movies. It was crazy. Getting noticed, as you know, is almost impossible. Darren and I fell in love with this one kid that played most of the lead roles in the community center back in Detroit where we were from, but couldn't catch a break. I don't know, we just came together... the three of us and figured it out. After that, Darren and I picked up and moved here to LA with the guy and started our careers as agents. He was with us until he died in a plane crash on the way to a set." She gave me a look. "Sorry. Maybe I shouldn't have-"

"No, it's fine." I awarded her with a warm smile. "I figure if this thing is going down, there isn't much I can do about it."

"True dat." She laughed. "Anyway, after that, I contracted another big name actor, and because of the hours we were spending together, I fell in love with him. He was good at what he did, if you know what I mean. Acting the part, that is." She glanced down as shame filled her face.

"It's easy to be fooled by someone that doesn't have skills. Someone that does? Impossible to get away unscathed, right?"

"Yes." She wiped at her eyes. "Anyway, I left Darren for him, and when that relationship fell apart a few weeks later, I decided I was working with females of any age or boys only from then on. No more seductive men for me."

She glanced up and smiled as Ethan walked toward us. "This turd was the first one they handed me, and seeing that he's still a kid... I'm safe."

Ethan sat down across the aisle from us and leaned forward to look at Deza. "You'll always be safe with me. Duh."

I chuckled and let myself relax a little more in the presence of the strangers who would soon become like family. I turned my face back toward Deza. "Did Darren not give you another chance?"

"What? You told Riley about you and Darren and you didn't tell me?" Ethan let out a childish sigh, and I chuckled, but kept my eyes on Deza.

"He was heartbroken, as he should have been. We couldn't even look at each other for four or five years, me from shame and him from anger." She shrugged. "Life became a competition after that for a while where we were going after the same performers. After a while, I backed off and mostly focused on Ethan."

"Smart move." Ethan leaned forward, and I turned to let my eyes run over his handsome face.

"I'd say so." I rolled my eyes and leaned back in my seat as the pilot came over the loud speaker and asked for his co-pilot to get in there and Frank to sit down.

I laughed and closed my eyes, letting out a soft sigh.

"You need me to hold your hand?" Ethan's voice was soft, but teasing.

"No," Deza barked and leaned forward as I opened my eyes to see what had gotten into her. "I'll hold her hand. Behave yourself."

I glanced between the two of them. "Something I should know about?"

Frank dropped down on the other side of Ethan and waved at me. "Morning, girls. You excited?"

Ethan shook his head and leaned back. "There's nothing to know. Deza promised to be open-minded about something I wanted to do, but as usual, she lied."

"I'm going to come over there and strangle your scrawny white ass if you don't stop." She leaned across me and swatted at him.

"Okay. Well, things are normal if nothing else." Frank smiled at me over the top of Ethan's head as he swatted at Deza's hand. "This is how they always act. You'll get used to it. They'll kiss and make up shortly. Gotta get the tension out from time to time."

"I see that." I swatted both of their hands away and crossed my arms over my chest as I closed my eyes.

"Did you say you quit your job?" Frank had to be talking to me.

I turned and opened my eyes, realizing that getting a nap was probably out. "Yeah. I quit before the party last week, though I shouldn't have."

"Why not?" Ethan snorted. "You couldn't have made much of anything. It was a waste."

"A waste that paid my bills. I've yet to get my advance on the movie and honestly don't know the timing of anything because my agent isn't really an agent." My tone had darkened a little thanks to the tension in the air.

"Then tell Deza to find out for you. You don't need to concern yourself with silly shit like a restaurant job or school, really. Why are you still trying to graduate? You've done what most people could only dream of doing." He lifted his hands dramatically.

How I could feel like I was falling off the cliff of love with him one minute and wanting to pick up rocks and stone him to death the next was confusing, but it was the truth. He looked so cute in his t-shirt and jeans when he'd walked onto the plane all puffed up. Now there was very little attractive about him as he acted flippantly about my life.

"It might be a matter of principle, Ethan." Frank leaned forward and winked at me. "I'm proud of you for wanting to graduate. It's been a long three years I bet."

"Yes, it has. I want to say I completed the journey. With it only a few months away, I plan to."

"Just don't let it get in the way of your performance. It's not worth that." Ethan crossed his arms over his chest and gave me a cocky look. Was he pissed at me or Deza? Sure felt like his directed aggression was being shifted from her to me.

"I'm aware of that, but being raised in poverty, saying that I have a college degree and knowing that I had to use scholarships to get there is a big deal. Some of us weren't raised on a silver spoon." I shouldn't have, but I couldn't help it.

"Oh, fuck," Deza mumbled beside me.

Had I hit a nerve? Good. I hoped I would. He was being a cock to D and now to me. Frank was up next, no doubt.

Ethan's expression tightened, aging him quickly. Handsome didn't hold a candle to how good he looked in the moment. Something about the way he watched me in his anger unraveled my insides.

I got up from my seat as the plane took off and walked to the back, whispering, "Excuse me."

My hands shook as I pulled down a bottle of whiskey from the cabinet above the flight attendant's work station. I'd filled up my glass halfway and was working to get ice in the cup when the delicious scent of Ethan's cologne wrapped around me.

"That wasn't fair." His voice was soft as he stood just behind me.

I turned and lifted my glass before taking a quick sip and groaning as it burned its way down my chest.

"Nope, nothing is fair in love and war, right?" I offered him a smile, but he didn't return it.

"I didn't come from a silver spoon. That's a shitty assumption to make." He took my glass, finished the liquor and took a step toward me. "You don't know anything about me. No one does."

"And that is because you refuse to share yourself." I poked my finger into his chest and moved around him. "Maybe you need to work on getting a bigger cock cup."

He snorted and glanced over his shoulder. "Always about my dick."

"I wasn't referring to your dick." I paused and glanced over my shoulder. "I was talking about something big enough to hide your personality when it goes from pleasant to shit in a moment's notice."

Chapter 11

Ethan

She fell asleep a few minutes later as I sat in the seat next to her, steaming. I was so pissed at Deza for being an ass about me and Riley sharing ourselves with each other. Was it dangerous? Yes, but so was humping the next stranger I ran into when we got off the plane.

Why everyone had to complicate everything was beyond me.

Silver spoon. Anger burned through me, causing my skin to heat and a slight sheen of sweat to collect at my brow and above my lip. My parents hadn't been around enough for us to have spoons. It was a miracle that Liam and I not only made it out of our childhood alive, but that we made something of ourselves. We were nothing but tools to two money-hungry people with the hope of grandeur and more greed than anyone should have to bear.

"You okay? You're sweating." Frank pressed his shoulder to mine and watched me with concern.

"I'm good. Just not feeling too hot." I stood and smiled down at him. "Or maybe feeling too hot. Just a little fever I guess. I'll be okay."

"Let me know if you need me. Go splash your face with cold water." He gave me a fatherly smile and leaned back in his seat.

I glanced over at the girls to find Riley still asleep, looking like an angel, and Deza staring out the window.

"Hey. I'm sorry." I reached over Riley and brushed my fingers down D's shoulder. "I'm just tense with all the shit going on. You know I suck at change."

"I'm sorry too. Love you." She reached out and gripped my hand, brushing her cheek by it. "You running a fever?"

She started to get up, but I motioned for her to stay still.

"I'm good. Just a little hot is all. I'll be all right. Stay there." I turned and walked toward the back of the plane as I forced my anger and hurt back into the tight box I kept them in. It was no one's fault that I'd suffered some crazy shit as a kid. I'd almost take it all again to keep the relationship Liam and I had forged out of the madness.

A shiver ran through me as I walked into the moderate-sized bathroom and turned on the cool water. After splashing water on my face several times, I dropped down on the toilet and let my head fall back.

Deza was right. Offering myself to Riley was fucking stupid, but it didn't matter much. The pretty girl hadn't taken me up on it, nor had she mentioned it again. She was too focused on keeping her old life intact and moving into a new one. I couldn't blame her. I'd not have diverged from the path to reach superstardom for anything a few years back. Now it felt like a ball and chain most days.

"Hey. You okay?" Riley's voice was filled with concern as she knocked on the door.

"Yeah. Just feeling a little feverish." I reached up and unlocked the door.

She opened it and moved to stand in the opening. "You look like shit."

I chuckled and closed my eyes. "Awesome."

"Well, you look incredible, but your looking like shit is someone else's best day." The sound of the water starting brought an odd calm over me.

"I'm fine." I blinked slowly as my heart slowed down a little. I was fine until she moved to squat in front of me. She was too close, the scene was too intimate. I could almost hear the porn music cued in the backdrop of my thoughts.

"You don't look fine." She reached up and ran the cold rag over my cheek as her face filled with concern.

"I'm good. I can do that." I wrapped my hand around hers and groaned as my stomach contracted painfully. Maybe I wasn't as good as I thought. "Get out."

I move up and knocked her over, not stopping to pick her up as I turned and pulled the toilet seat up as my breakfast came back up. I gripped the sides of the seat and groaned again as I moved down to my knees.

"Ethan. What can I do?" Her voice was so soft.

"Nothing." I wanted to care that the finest girl in my world was standing behind me while I barfed my guts out, but nothing mattered other than getting through the moment.

The brush of the soft rag against the back of my neck calmed me. I panted softly and sat back on my heels as she tugged at the bottom of my shirt.

"Take this off." Her voice drove a spike of desire past my sickness and caused the room to grow fuzzy.

"Trying to get me naked while I'm out of it, I see." I lifted my arms as she pulled the shirt off and knelt behind me. The soft swipe of the cold rag in her hand felt good against my hot skin. I pressed my arms to the toilet and rested my head against them.

"What happened? What's the matter?" Deza's voice was loud, aggravating.

I groaned again and lifted up to my knees to start another round of vomiting.

"He's not doing so well." Riley sounded worried.

It was odd to have her taking care of me. I'd long given up on finding anyone other than Deza and Liam that would be something special in my life. She was going to whittle her way down into my heart. I could tell that I wouldn't have a standing chance if she tried.

"Get out," I groaned again and swatted at them wildly. "Seriously. Fuck."

"I'm out. He turns into a diva when he's sick." Deza snorted.

"I'm not going anywhere, you ass. Just get it out and let me take care of you." Riley's fingernails dragged over my back.

I moaned and pressed my hands to my face as I tried to catch my breath. "That feels good."

"Good. Just breathe through your nose. Long, slow breaths." Her finger brushed down my spine followed by the cold rag as she pressed it open and coated my skin in its coolness.

"You're making me want to be nice all the time. Stop." I pursed my lips as my stomach revolted against the peace she was working to help me find.

"Stop being cheeky and breathe. You can be an ass when we get out of here and you're feeling better."

I wanted her arms around me. Wanted to feel her lips against my ear and the soft press of her cheek against my skin. I wanted more than I should have wanted. It was unfair to either of us to even give voice to my needs or her desires. To mix the two would be explosive in the moment, and then much like a bomb going off, we would be left with the aftermath to clean up.

"I'm better." I sat back again and blinked through the haze around me. "Can you get me a sprite or water?"

"Of course." She stood up and walked out of the bathroom as I sagged against the wall to my left. "Here. Small sips."

I took the drink and moved back to my ass. "Thank you."

"Of course." She leaned over and flushed the toilet before kneeling beside me again. Her pretty pink top accentuated the feminine features I'd come to enjoy seeing. Her little button nose and luscious full lips. Caring blue eyes and flawless skin.

I reached out and brushed the back of my fingers down the side of her face as I lifted the cup to my lips. "Tell me Jace isn't your man. Lie to me."

"Hush. Don't start this Casanova shit again." She picked up the wet towel beside the sink and moved closer, wiping at the side of my face. "You're just not feeling good."

"True, but still. You deserve a good man."

"Do those exist?" She gave me a cheeky grin and fuck if I didn't want to reach out and pull her into my lap. I felt like hell was waging war on my stomach, but kissing her sounded like the best-laid plan I could devise. She's taken care of me. I wanted to return the favor.

"I'm not sure to be honest." I took the towel from her and pressed it to my head. "I think I'm good. Honestly. Thank you for taking care of me."

"We promised each other that we would protect the other. This is just an extension of that, right?" She moved back and stood up before offering her hand. "Let me help you up."

"I'm too big." I set my sprite on the counter above me and gripped the side of the sink.

She huffed at me. "You are not. Give me your damn hand, you lug."

"See. You just called me a lug." I gave her my hand and let her half pull me up. The room spun, and I reached out and gripped her arm with my free hand. "Fuck. I have no clue what I ate, but never again."

"Come on. Let's get you back in your seat." She pulled me out of the bathroom and wrapped her arm around the back of my waist, letting me lean on her a little.

"How the hell did that go from bad to worse so fast?" I mumbled and sat down in my seat as Frank stiffened next to me.

"What's wrong? Did you get sick?" He took the sprite from Deza, who must have gone to get it for me.

"I'm good. Just something I ate." I leaned back and reclined my chair. "I'm going to take a nap. Wake me up when we get there."

"Rest up. We're not doing anything today, but I do want us to have a mini-scene camp tomorrow before the big scene shooting gets underway. Nothing too crazy, but just a few things on technique and style, especially for you, Riley."

I waved my hand in the air to get him to shut up. "We'll get it down. Hush so I can rest. Hopefully whatever was fucking me up is over."

Riley pressed the wet cloth to my head as I glanced up at her and caught her wrist.

"Thank you. Seriously." I brought her hand to my mouth and kissed her wrist softly. "I needed that."

Her cheek turned pink as Frank grumbled next to me. I didn't care.

"Sure. Of course." She pulled her hand from me and walked to her seat, dropping down with a sigh. "Just get some sleep."

"Don't let Frank molest me. He's had the hots for me for years." I smiled as he laughed beside me.

"He's going to be fine. He's already acting like himself again."

Funny they would know what the real me looked like. I hadn't seen him in years, but for a moment in the bathroom, with Riley behind me, taking care of me... I almost felt him. Almost.

Chapter 12

Riley

We flew throughout the night, and Ethan barely moved through the whole event. Not even when we hit a pretty bad storm near the end of the trip. It was almost lunchtime the next day in Rio when we finally got off the plane. I'd never been so glad to see solid ground before. Not being someone who'd flown more than once in my life, I'd held it together pretty well through the whole ordeal. Having to help Ethan was almost a godsend. It kept my attention on him and not on my worries about being in the air for so long.

I'd tried to sound like a Billy-bad-ass with Deza the day before like dying on the plane was all part of the risk, and was no big deal. Truth be told, I was terrified and hiding it like I did everything else.

"It's beautiful here." Ethan moved up beside me, looking a little too pale still.

"Yeah. How are you?" I turned to face him and reached out to press the back of my fingers to his forehead. "You feel good."

"You ain't seen nothing yet, baby doll." He winked and turned as Deza moved up beside us.

"All right. We have two small cars coming to take us to the beach condo we rented. You boys ride together and me and Riley will ride together. We get the first car that comes though. I need a shower or I'm going to turn into a class-A witch." Deza gave us a look as if to compound her words with truth.

"Turn into? What are you now?" Ethan chuckled and lifted his hands as she moved to pop him. "Be careful with the goods please. I'm feeling better, but I'm not nearly one hundred percent yet."

"You'll be better by tomorrow. We have the rest of the afternoon to lay around the condo, or soak up the sun for those of us who are desperate for a tan." Frank pulled up the sleeve of his Hawaiian shirt and we all flinched.

"Oh the agony of the whiteness." Ethan turned and acted as if he were ducking from a nuclear blast. "That's bad, man."

"I told you." Frank chuckled. "Here is car one. You girls go ahead."

"Unless you want to go with Deza and I'll ride with Frank. I know you're not feeling good." I turned my attention to Ethan.

"No. I'll be all right. Really." He smiled. "You're being too sweet for your own good. I wanna marry you instead of just turn you into my bedroom toy. Be careful, woman. You'll get yourself in too deep."

"Does he use these lines on everyone?" Frank snorted.

"Nope. I'm going to give Riley the down low in the car. She's in trouble and the boy has hearts in his eyes."

"Hey. We're right here." Ethan winked at me. "Hearts in my eyes? Dumb. You guys are old."

It was interesting how open everyone was with one another. I wasn't sure if I would ever get there, but it was fun to watch the others in action.

"Yes, well, I'm taking my old ass to the condo." Deza moved toward the car as Ethan motioned for me to join her.

"I'm good. Go to the condo. I'll find you tonight and we can have a drink or something." His eyes moved across my face as if memorizing me. How easily it would have been to fall in love with him.

I was lying if I thought I wasn't already there, but was it him that I was in love with, or his talent? Or the parts he played, even better yet?

"All right. Thanks." I rolled my bag to the small car, and thanked the driver for loading it for us.

Deza was resting with her eyes closed when I got in. I didn't want to bother her, so I pulled out my phone and worked through the text messages I had from Charlotte. She was about the only one I spoke with. It would seem that my boss from the restaurant had called a few times in the last day to apologize for being so harsh with me. Funny how people realized just how good they had it, but only when it was gone.

"Did Ethan offer you a friends with benefits-type relationship?" Her voice caught me off-guard.

"Hm? No. I don't think so." Embarrassment raced through me. He's hinted at it, but I couldn't really tell if he were being cheeky or honestly wanted me to come to him when I was horny and away from home. It seemed far too casual for my liking.

"You sure? You can tell me, you know." She pinned me with a hard stare.

"He might have mentioned it, but honestly, I figured he was just kidding."

"Right, well, he wasn't." She rolled her eyes. "I swear that boy is going to be the death of me."

"Did he mention it to you?" Horror raced through me that they were *that* open. The teasing and picking at Ethan about his man-parts and stuff, I could get used to. Getting into the intimate details of my sex life? Not so much.

"Yes! Yes, child. He wanted to make sure I was good with it." She pressed her hands to her face. "He has absolutely no sense of modesty at all. You should be warned. If you were on one film with us, no biggie, but knowing that you're most likely going to do three? That's three to four years of working together. Be warned."

I forced a laugh and leaned back, turning my face to look out the window as we passed the busy city and headed out to the water. She seemed to take the hint that I was done talking for the moment, and I was grateful for the silence.

I didn't know how I felt about him mentioning to Deza a friends with benefits relationship between us. Where the idea of stripping him naked and making him moan was something I could find at the edge of my desires, it was a risk. A risk I wasn't sure I was ready to take. My daydreams were more than enough for now, and even though getting sweaty and rolling around in the sheets with him was inevitable, I was going to hang on for as long as I could. Hopefully.

"I'm going to the beach for a while. You wanna come?" Deza stood by the front door with her sunglasses on and towel draped over her arm.

"No, I'm good. I'm going to read for a while. I'll find you later." I offered her a warm smile and turned onto my side as I pulled up Ethan's bio on my phone. It seemed almost like snooping around, and yet I couldn't help it. He wasn't going to give up too much information from what I could tell. He protected himself almost to the extent that I did.

"No wonder he doesn't have anyone close in his life but those that work beside him." And his brother. Thinking of Liam brought a smile to my lips. He'd been so entertaining on the boat ride out to Catalina Island the weekend before. He and Ethan had the type of relationship I'd want if I had a brother or sister. The thought of my brother Derick brushed across my thoughts, but as always, I dismissed it quickly. Too much sadness surrounded it to let it penetrate my soul and bring me down.

I switched to my texts and shot my mother another one. It would be the fifth one in the last week without a reply from her. I was worried, but there wasn't much I could do until she returned my calls or sent me a text back.

"Not gonna worry about it. I've been waiting for this big break half my life." I flipped it back to Ethan's bio as a knock resounded at the door. I groaned softly and got up, half-expecting it to be Deza.

Ethan stood on the other side of the door in a pair of swim trunks, sandals and a bright pink towel over his shoulders. "Come down to the water with me."

"Deza just went down. Go find her. I wanted to read for a while."

"Nope. I want time with you. You saved my life yesterday. The least I can do is buy you dinner and a drink." He moved around me into the room. "This is nice. Why are you guys sharing a room? The house is huge. It's almost like a mini apartment complex."

"This is the only room with two beds. We figured it would be easier for us to share a room than to get one of the film crew guys to share rooms." I shrugged and walked into the room, letting the door close behind me. "I'll go down for dinner, but I'm not very hungry."

"We'll share something." He pulled my white bikini from my open suitcase. "Wear this. I like it."

I laughed and snagged it from his fingers. "I don't care what you like. I'm wearing what I have on."

"You can't get wet like that. Well, you can, but not the way that would keep us both safe." He sucked in a deep breath and ran his eyes along me.

Chill bumps broke out along my skin as my body tightened due to his nearness. I reached out and gripped his wrist, pulling him toward the door.

"Let's go. Out of my bedroom."

"This is new. I've never in my life heard those words put into one congruent sentence together." He offered me his arm, and I would have been an ass for not taking it.

"Stop being cute. It's getting on my nerves." I smiled at him as we moved down the hall and out the side exit of the condo.

"Would you rather I be an ass?" He released my arm and touched the small of my back as we moved through a crowd of people. They whispered something which included his name. "Damn. I thought we were staying on a private island."

"We are." I glanced around. "I don't see many people here. They're probably part of the camera crew. New movie, new people working for you guys, right?"

"That's true." He seemed to accept my explanation and relaxed again. "Thanks again for helping me yesterday."

"Of course. Are you feeling better?" I wrapped my arms around myself and glanced up as the sun sat near the water's edge. It was going to be a beautiful sunset, but felt a little too romantic beside him.

"Much better." He glanced toward the water. "Look... the sun's going to almost look like it bursts when it hits the water. Let's go watch." He gripped my hand and moved us out there as tension drove me toward silence. "Beautiful."

"Can I ask you something?" I looked up at him as my heart shuddered in my chest.

"Anything." He glanced down at me and turned back to watch the sunset. "Just don't ask me to marry you. It's too soon, and I'm not sure we're compatible in the bedroom. If you wanna have dinner and use each other for dessert just to make sure everything fits in its proper place, you can hit your knees afterward."

"Hit my knees?" I yelped and popped him in the chest as he laughed loudly. The expression on his face stole a part of my heart and left me weak.

"To ask me to marry you. Shit... I didn't mean." He lifted his eyebrow. "Well, that would be fucking awesome too, but-"

I hit him again.

"But... that's not what I meant." He reached out and slid his strong hands over my shoulders. "Ask me the question."

"Why did you deny me the kiss at your house? Was it because you had someone else coming over for the night?" I tried to remain calm, though everything inside of me prepared for the worst. There was no good answer. Either way I looked at it, he'd slept with the pretty girl and kicked me out. Rejection stung the center of my chest like I was right back there again.

"It was a test, right?"

"No. It wasn't." I glanced out at the sunset. "I lied to save face. I'd not been rejected too many times in my life. It was a first and it was embarrassing. I covered it up."

Was I really being this honest with him? Ugh. I hated myself.

He slid his hands up my neck and cupped my face, forcing me to look at him.

"I did it out of respect for you, and for me. Deza asked that I stay hands off with you because whatever is happening between us needs to happen for a long time. I'm horrible with relationships, so I figured it would be a respectable thing to do, but the minute I did it... I regretted it. I just knew one kiss wasn't enough."

"Am I talking with the real Ethan Lewis?" I smiled and cupped my hands over his, finding a warmth in his embrace that I'd almost expected *not* to be there.

"I'm the one and only." He brushed his thumbs over my cheeks. "Forgive me for denying us both? I'm afraid they expect me to keep doing that."

"And it's probably smart that you do." I pulled his hands off of me as the sound of voices stole my attention.

"Oh, shit." He put his back to me as a huge group of girls jogged down the beach toward us, all of them yelling his name. "Private doesn't exist anymore, does it?"

"Go get 'em tiger." I popped his butt and turned to walk back up toward the drink hut.

"You're not leaving me here. Seriously?"

I laughed all the way to my barstool, where I sat for the next hour waiting on him. A whole host of emotions ran through me, but by the time he dropped down beside me, I was sure of one thing.

I was also glad that he hadn't kissed me. God only knew where we would be if he had.

Chapter 13

Ethan

"Oh my God! Ethan Lewis. You're my favorite actor of all time. I've loved you since I could walk!"

The women seemed to be multiplying like gremlins as the ocean water sprayed us with a light mist. I glanced over my shoulder, praying that Riley had come back to save me, but she was long gone. Not that I blamed her. As much as I appreciated my fans for buying tickets to my movies, I wanted the relationship to have a big-ass movie screen separating their greedy fingers and my body.

"Aww... thanks. I appreciate that more than you know." I signed a few more papers, bags and purses, and a few sets of tits before I could get away. How women knew to carry a Sharpie with them wherever they went was a mystery I wouldn't soon figure out.

I finally wrapped up things with them, denied the free dinners and blow jobs and walked back up toward the cantina, where Riley was nursing a beer.

"What is your definition of private? I'm thinking Frank and Deza have a completely different idea of what a private, secluded beach looks like. That, or they fucking hate me." I sat down on the bar stool beside her and ordered a Corona when the bartender stopped in front of us.

She laughed and ran her eyes over me, leaving my attention only for her, once again.

"Private is relative, right?" She lifted her beer to her lips and took a long drink.

"Private honestly doesn't exist when you live in the eye of the public. I know Deza was hoping that I would mentor you a little, so consider that lesson one. Honestly. Anything you do, have done or are contemplating doing, the world will know about it, and the press will be hot on your ass to get the gory details and publish it."

She paled a little. "Great."

"Yeah. It sucks. Just be ready. If you have anything in your past that-"

"I do." She turned back toward the bar and glanced down. "I have a lot of poverty, a mother that acts like a fifteen-year-old slut and a brother that was killed in a drive-by because of shitty choices. I'm sure the rags to riches story is going to be touted across the airways before we can blink twice."

I tucked the information away to dissect that and simply nodded and pressed my forearms to the bar in front of me. I'd never have guessed that she had such a fucked up family life. That had to be where some of her high emotion came from during our scenes. "Unfortunately it is. My situation with my folks has been aired enough times that the media refer to me as the star with no beginning." I snorted. "As if I popped up from an underwater aquifer and started living the life of a movie star."

She glanced over at me as a smile tugged at the side of her perfect mouth. "It's funny because I've been watching you grow up on screen most of my life, and I honestly can't remember a mention of your mom and dad."

"That's because we keep them in the closet with the rest of the skeletons." I winked at her and lifted my beer to my lips. "You know, I wonder..."

She turned, brushing her knee by my thigh as she put her full attention on me. I enjoyed the weight of it almost too much. My body hardened, but it was nothing new around her.

"Tell me what you wonder."

"Those girls down there..." I glanced over my shoulder praying they hadn't crept up the beach like something out of a horror film. "Some of them had me sign their breasts. Do you think guys ask female actors to sign their dicks or do they just use paper?"

"That is an interesting thought. I'll let you know whenever it happens. I'd assume it's probably their chests or paper, right?" Her cheeks turned a light shade of pink, though she seemed unaffected otherwise. "Speaking of dicks..."

"Man, I'm falling in love with you. What other chick has a conversation starter that most men would die to hear the rest of?" I laughed as she chuckled and swatted at my chest. She was beyond beautiful. It took everything inside of me not to reach out and drag her in for a long, hard kiss. My patience was running thin on having her in my bed and it hadn't been more than a few weeks since we'd met. If I were playing the good guy part that Deza wanted me to play, that moment would never come, nor would I.

"Did you tell Deza that you wanted to have a friends with benefits relationship with me?"

It felt like ice water got tossed in my face. It was like being in the throes of talking dirty with a woman and she mentioned having babies together. My happy, rock-solid boner dropped like the stock market during the Great Depression.

"No." I gave her a silly look like *she* was the idiot. "I mean, I might have mentioned that I was joking with you about sleeping with me if you needed a good, long, hard-"

"Okay. I get it." She narrowed her eyes in a way that had my dick rising back to attention. The woman was going to give my crotch pneumonia. Up and down. Up and down. "She doesn't seem like the type to twist the truth."

"She's not, but... she is a girl." I licked at my lips and took another drink of my beer. "You guys have been known to skew the truth in your favor, bend words to get your way and twist thoughts of the most unsuspecting males to end up where you wanted to."

"No way. Guys are way worse than women at all of that." She wagged her eyebrows.

"Nope. That takes far too much effort for a dude. We just tell it like it is and take cover under the nearest bomb shelter. Life's too short to pussy-foot around, right?"

"True. So you did mention it to her."

"Kinda, not really." I shrugged. "In all honesty, I might have laid the idea before her just in case she flew off the handle and didn't like it. I was teasing you when I mentioned it, but after thinking it through, I really liked the idea."

"Because you want to protect each other." She was leading me down a dark path and looked like Goldilocks doing it. Sweet, innocent, hot as fucking sin. Women like her were the reason most men *thought* they were going to end up at the pearly gates only to drop down into the smoking section. Trickery had to be her calling card, but regardless... I was in it to win it. At least for a night.

"Absolutely. You don't want crotch-rot, do you? I hear sexually transmitted diseases are a bitch. Or how about someone starting a fan club and talking about what a piece of shit you are?" I finished off my beer and tried not to dive too deep into my own horror show that played in my head. If I had any piece of advice that I could back up with loads of painful personal experience, it was not to sleep with strangers. It never turned out well.

"Maybe I'm the kind of girl who doesn't need sex, Ethan. Just because you seem to thrive on it doesn't mean the rest of us do."

"Thrive on it?" I laughed. "Let's be honest here. I haven't had a proper fucking in the last two to three years."

"Really? Why is that?" She got up and motioned for me to join her.

Had I really opened up the conversation to talk about the one thing that left me feeling inadequate as a male altogether? My brother could joke about it all day long, and I understood quite well how fucking stupid it sounded when I spoke it out loud, but my dick was too big. In a way that left me without any measure of pleasure far more often than not.

We walked to the edge of the water in silence and sat down in the sand as the moonlight bathed the shore in its ethereal light.

"Well? Tell me." She slid her hand behind her and tilted her head toward me. The position jutted out her breasts.

My mouth grew dry and nervousness raced through the center of my chest. What the hell was it with this woman? She shouldn't have had the power to intimidate me, but she did. It was a turn on nevertheless, so I was willing to put up with it to the point of being uncomfortable.

"You tell me that Jace is your boyfriend that you're in love with and would never cheat on first, and I'll explain a little bit of my shit to you." I ran my hand through my hair and glanced back at the ocean. The sound of the waves crashing on the shore brought a balm to my soul that I didn't realize I needed. Maybe the trip would do me some good.

"How are you feeling? Your stomach okay?" She turned her attention back to the water and looked up at the sky.

"What? You're so horrible at transitions when deflecting. We need to work on this. You gotta treat it like a scene in a movie. So, like, if I didn't want to answer the question about Jace, I would have said, boyfriends are a difficult topic. They sometimes make you feel like a million bucks, and sometimes make you feel like barfing up your guts. Hey... speaking of barfing up your guts." I glanced over at her. "How are you feeling from earlier? Your stomach okay?"

She laughed and pressed her shoulder to mine. "I don't care if the transition is horrible. The end result is the same. He's none of your business."

"I agree, but I'm just asking about the relationship. Anyone could ask that. Fuck, they will. I promise. I'm just trying to see if you're locked into something good and solid with the guy."

"And if I am?" Her eyes moved across my face slowly.

She might be with him, but she wasn't with him. There was no way. She was far too much woman for the playboy-looking jock.

"Then I'll leave you alone about being fuck-buddies." I shrugged and turned back toward the water. "I think we'd be quite compatible in the bedroom."

"Do you now?" She moved up to her hands and knees and pulled something from the sand. A seashell. "And you really think I can do something with that monster you're packing?" Her smile was contagious, but her words drove deep into the center of me.

"Monster. Right." I got up and stretched, trying not to let the moment drown in my own issues, and yet failing miserably. "I'm going to grab some crackers and head back to my room. This was fun. I'll see you in the morning for rehearsal."

"What?" She looked up with a tense expression. "Why are you going?"

"I'm tired." I turned and walked toward the condo as anger swirled in the pit of my stomach. I was quite proud of myself for not barking out some nasty comment about having to pet the monster alone.

A friends with benefits relationship with Riley would have been the perfect answer to both of our problems, but until I figured out how to shrink my shit and she stopped pretending that the thing between her and Channing Tatum's twin was anything more than an occasional romp in the sheets, it wasn't happening.

Funny enough, the worst part of realizing that was coming to terms with the fact that Deza was getting her way without even trying. I growled low in my chest as I walked into the cool air of the house and paused.

I was in Rio and we weren't on a private beach at all. I wasn't going to bed like a little old man. Nursing my wounded ego would feel much better. All I needed was a six pack of beer and a hot woman. Both couldn't be too hard to find.

Chapter 14

Riley

I laid in bed half the night trying to figure out what I'd done to offend Ethan. I'd gone through the denial stages first, as if surely I hadn't done anything and he was being an overly sensitive tit. So I didn't want to talk about Jace, and I didn't want to dive into a relationship with him that would leave me heartbroken by the morning.

Deza slipped out of the room just after the sun rose, and I found myself still staring at the window, wide awake. I needed to figure out what I'd done and apologize for it, though I hated to. It would seem Ethan was nothing more than an immature ass and I would have to be the bigger person throughout our time together.

Outside of all that drama, I still couldn't believe that I was getting ready to shoot a movie with Ethan Lewis. He was America's crush. Butterflies danced around in my chest as I rolled onto my back and closed my eyes. It would be so nice if he was the strong personality in real life that he was in his Bond films. The demanding, get-in-my-bed-and-let-me-fuck-you-senseless kind of man we all imagined him to be, and maybe he was, but he was going about it all wrong.

Offering me a contract-like agreement to be fuck-buddies? Why not just take me to bed and explain that it's just physical before we did the dirty? I laughed at the thought. There really was no good way around it. He wanted what Jace and I had, and a huge part of me didn't want to deny him. We were in very different places. I was a complete stranger that had moved onto his side of the street, and he was someone I'd been watching forever.

Damn I loved watching him. His dark brown hair and sexy brown eyes. The thickness of his bottom lip and his perfectly regal nose.

A tendril of pleasure shot through my stomach as I groaned in the early morning light. Need pumped through me, and I lifted my head, listening to make sure Deza had actually left and not come back in the middle of my internal ramblings.

I closed my eyes and exhaled softly before sliding my hands down my stomach and pushing my panties over my hips. I hadn't taken care of myself in forever, but with a wicked hot fantasy playing in my head, and Ethan being center stage to it, I needed to.

His hands were firm on the sides of my neck and he glanced down the long length of our bodies and smiled. "Fuck, you look good. So beautiful and soft. I wanna hear you scream."

I groaned and ran my hands down his side as he pressed me to the bed and hovered above me, looking like a god in the early morning light.

"Then make me." I lifted my head as he swooped down and licked at my mouth. I wrapped my hands around the back of his head and held him in place as he worked his tongue deep into my mouth and rolled his hips enough to settle the thick head of his cock between my legs.

"You sure you can handle me?" He brushed his lips by mine and moved to press his elbows into the bed just beside my head.

Every cell in my body was lit up with desire for the man above me. He didn't seem at all uncomfortable or unsure of himself. He was every hot fantasy I'd had over the years.

"I'm more than capable of handling you." There was no fear or worry about him not fitting. We'd make it work. I wanted to. I

coveted his size and wanted to be the woman he found relief and pleasure with.

My hips arched forward as I brushed my fingers through the wet folds of my skin and groaned. Chill bumps broke out on my skin, leaving me panting before I got too far. It'd been too long. Jace and I hadn't had time to fuck the week before after the opening celebration for *Down Low*, though I needed to something terrible.

"Why do I believe that?" He pressed into me a little and smiled. "Spread your legs wider, Riley. Open up like a good girl for me."

I groaned and spread my thighs farther as I slid my hands over his thick shoulders and pressed up to take more of him.

The pleasure that spread across his face as he laid down and pressed me firmly to the mattress was bliss, beautiful.

"So tight, baby. So deliciously tight and wet." He licked the side of my throat and rocked his hips, forcing me to take more and more of him. The pressure was overwhelming, and left me breathless.

I cried out as I sunk two fingers into myself and arched my back to get the best position for working my body over the edge as fast as I could. The idea of taking him deep inside was unbelievably appetizing, almost like a fetish. I enjoyed bigger men, but had never in my life seen anything like what Ethan was sporting. Monster was an understatement.

I worked harder and faster, slipping in another finger and giving myself over to the depravity of a hard fuck in my head as I pressed more aggression than I normally would have into my movement. I buckled in the bed as bright lights exploded at the edge of my vision. I rolled onto my side and continued to massage my soft skin as the high rolled into a warmth I yearned for.

Panting softly in the dark, I couldn't help but wonder if he went to bed the night before and did the same. After our conversation and him getting upset, I couldn't fathom a different ending for him.

After taking a quick shower, I put on a pair of white shorts and a blue tank top set, strapped sandals on my feet and walked down to the kitchen to find Frank and Deza talking to a guy I hadn't met yet. He had a scraggly beard, but brilliant blue eyes.

"Riley. Did you sleep well?" Deza got up and walked to the coffee pot.

"I didn't, actually. Not sure what's up with me." I smiled at the new guy and Frank. "Morning."

"Morning, youngin'." Frank pointed to the guy. "This is Paul. He's going to be our head videographer. He's a shy guy, but I'm sure you'll pull him from his shell."

The guy laughed and extended his hand toward me. "Nice to meet you, and please leave me in my shell. It's warm and cozy and safe."

I smiled and shook his hand. "You got another one of those shells? I think I need one too."

Deza offered me a cup of coffee. "Here you go. No shells for anyone. We're all going to gel and have a great time becoming a family."

"Hopefully better than the one I already have. If not, we're in trouble." I took the coffee and sat down beside Frank. "Where is Ethan?"

"He's a late sleeper." Frank nursed his coffee and stared at something absently across the kitchen. "He didn't get back to the house until early this morning either. I swear I'm going to have to put a curfew on him like we did when he was a teenager."

Deza snorted. "Good luck on that shit. He's more rebellious now than he was then."

"That can't be possible." Paul moved into the kitchen and pressed his hands to the other side of the counter from where we sat. "He's grown up some, right? At least since the last time I saw him."

"Not at bit." Deza laughed and took the seat on my right. "I wouldn't either if I were him. It's a hard life he lives. At least some of us get a break between filming one movie and the next. The poor kid is always Ethan Lewis no matter where he goes."

"And that's a bad thing?" Frank gave us a funny look. "You should have seen the woman he brought home with him last night. Playboy would pay her large sums of money to keep her clothes *on* and just smile for the camera. He's a lucky man, but he lets it go to his head."

The woman he brought home?

Sickness swirled in the pit of my stomach until it birthed anger and rejection. The logical side of my mind pushed the horrible thoughts away, but my emotions clung to all of it until I had a hard time finding enough air to breathe. He'd offered himself to me the night before and when I didn't jump into his bed, he ran out and got another woman? A woman that could have any host of diseases that he'd warned me of?

What a bastard. What a horrible, piece of shit bastard.

"So are you excited, Riley? First day of working on scenes for the new movie." Frank rubbed the top of my back and gave me a warm smile.

"What? Yeah. Oh yeah. I'm really excited." I took a sip of my coffee and slipped into character. I was a young woman who was ready to live out her dreams. I had a loving fiancé at home that called three times a day and was quick to remind me of all the naughty things he planned to do to me the minute I got back home from my trip. I could be her throughout the day until I crashed that night, hating myself for denying Ethan. I hated myself for hating myself.

I growled softly and got up.

"You okay?" Deza reached out and gripped my wrist.

"Yeah, just trying to think through why my mother isn't answering my calls. I haven't heard from her in a few days, which is nothing new." I shrugged. "I just wish I knew that she was okay."

"You need us to send someone to look for her? We have a good handful of people on the payroll back in Los Angeles." Frank's offer was kind, and a little humorous.

"You sound like you run the mafia." I changed my voice to sound like a mafia boss from Boston. "Yeah, uh, wez got people everywherez. Just name your price, pretty girl, and itz yours."

They all laughed, forcing a smile from me too.

"You're right where you should be. Obviously." Paul walked toward the hallway. "Which room is the golden boy staying in? I think I should give him a proper wake up call."

"Last door on the left," Frank called out. "Give him hell, please. It would make my day for sure."

"Behave." Deza popped Frank in the chest and turned to me. "Let's get over to the conference room down the beach. We'll be working there mostly today and then tomorrow we'll get on set. It's supposed to storm this afternoon, so we're holding off on setting up the props for the beach scenes."

"Sounds good." I took a few quick sips of my coffee and dumped the rest. I had to tuck away the fact that Ethan had taken a woman to his bed. I could analyze it later, but knew without a doubt that I would come to the sound conclusion that it was none of my business. He was a single guy with needs, and I wasn't his girl.

I was his co-star and nothing more. Me being the object of his affections was the same pipe dream that every girl with a pulse in America shared.

He was everything to everyone, and I was just me.

Somehow that didn't feel like nearly enough.

Chapter 15

Ethan

I ran my hand up the smooth skin of Vanessa's back and watched the sunrise, hating myself for trying again. The pretty thing lying beside me was dead to the world, and I was still without a proper release. She'd worked me with her hands several times, but it wasn't anything I couldn't have done myself.

How badly I wanted her to be Riley, to have the opportunity to take my time and open her up properly. Something told me that I would be much more patient with my beautiful co-star than I had been with the woman beside me. I'd finally given up at three that morning and rolled over, leaving her to cry beside me. I hated myself for it, but I couldn't seem to muster a nice thing to say.

"You awake?" she whispered and turned to face me. Her large breasts pressed against my chest as she curled up to the front of me. "You still mad at me?"

"I wasn't mad in the first place. Disappointed, yeah, but it's a normal occurrence in my life." I shrugged and brushed her dark hair from her shoulder.

Deza was right. I enjoyed white women with pale skin, but something had me going for the polar opposite the night before. I think I'd been scared to mistake her for Riley in any way, shape or form with my eyes wide open. Closing them and letting her become my latest obsession was fine, but pretending to have something I wanted only to fool myself was stupid. Childish.

"Let's try again. You still have a little while, right?" She ran her fingers down the side of my face and pulled me in for a kiss.

I wasn't in the mood to ever try again, but obviously my cock had a mind of its own. I ran my palm down her side, over the thick swell of her hip and gripped her ass, pulling her closer.

"Why do you think this morning will be any different than last night?" I nipped at her mouth as aggression pumped through me.

"I don't know. I want to make love to you. You're my fantasy." She pushed at my chest and crawled on top of me as I moved to my back and lifted one of my hands, sliding it under my head as I watched her.

She was beyond beautiful, and yet not my type in the slightest.

"I'm everyone's fantasy. That doesn't mean too much to me, you know?" I palmed her large tit and squeezed softly before tugging gently on her nipple. "Why don't you just suck me off? You know I'm not fitting inside of you."

"Maybe if you ate me out first. Then I would be ready." She pressed her hands into my chest and rolled her hips. The sweetness of having my cock coated in her wetness was a lie of things to come.

"Not happening, pretty girl." I gripped her hips and pulled her off of me. "Find me later tonight. I need some sleep before we start filming. The door is over there."

I turned on my side and pulled my pillow over my head as she bitched for the next five minutes about what a horrible guy I was. She was the one who'd approached me at the bar the night before, offered me a night I wouldn't forget and now she was pissed that her words rang true. I wouldn't forget that nothing happened out of the ordinary. The night sucked much like they all had.

I was done trying for a while unless there was a secondary purpose in it. Making Deza mad? That would be worth taking another useless woman to my bed. Pissing Frank off? Absolutely worth it. Making Riley jealous?

My stomach contracted as I groaned. I wanted to see her jealous and angry over me more than I wanted to find the right girl to take to my bed. I had so much to offer, but without the drive to offer it, I was nothing more than an asshole.

"Real men eat pussy." She pulled the pillow off my head and clocked me with it.

I laughed and rolled over the other way, pressing my face to the cool sheets below. I had a million comebacks about real women taking a dick properly, but I let them hide behind my closed lips. There was no need to degrade her any more than I already had by denying her another opportunity to come at my expense.

I rarely went down on a woman, simply because it felt almost too intimate. As odd as it sounded in my own head, I was saving something so intense for the right woman, and then I was going to give all I had.

The door closed, and I got up, walking to the bathroom and taking a long shower. I got back into the bed still wet and passed out without thinking too much about my last bad decision. I'd keep making them, no doubt, as I continued to search for something that felt so close and yet just out of my reach.

"Get up, buttercup!" Paul shook the bed and picked up my pillow, smacking me on the head with it several times.

"Get out, or I'll pimp slap you, and you know I'm capable of doing it." I swatted at him as I spoke through the thick haze of sleep.

"Keep that fire hose to yourself and get up. The girls are already headed to the conference room." He hit me a few more times and jumped backward as I got up and charged him. "Aww... man. You're naked. Really? Shit."

I released him and ran my fingers through my hair. "You filming this shit for us?"

Paul had to be one of my favorite crew members, but the man had mad skills. He was in high demand, and though we had him on the team for most of the early Bond films, he'd been picked up by several other production companies and we lost out. Frank had promised to work a new deal with him to get him back on the crew.

It would seem it worked.

"Obviously. Why does it smell like sex and candy in here?" He scrunched up his nose and shook his head as if he were disgusted.

"Breathe in deep, my friend. That's the smell of defeat. You wouldn't know." I laughed and walked to the dresser beside the television. After pulling on a pair of shorts and tugging a t-shirt over my head, we walked out and stopped by the kitchen. "Where is Frank?"

"He's probably with Riley and Deza." Paul opened the fridge and pulled out cold cuts and cheese as I made myself a travel mug of coffee.

"Speaking of Riley." I leaned against the counter, most likely looking like hell seeing that I felt like it. Good thing we were just working on scenes and not filming for the first day.

"Yeah." He made himself a sandwich while I watched, waiting for something more from him. "You want one?"

"Duh." I sat down and took a sip of my coffee. "So that's it? No comment on her looks or her personality or anything?"

He smiled and glanced up. "She's your kinda gal, isn't she? Short blond hair, funny, confident, great rack and intensely beautiful."

I nodded and breathed in deeply. "Yeah. She's the full package, man. I keep trying to get her into bed, but she won't have none of it."

"Has she seen what you're packing?" He chuckled as I gave him a look.

"It's always dick-envy with you." I took the sandwich he offered me and got up. "Let's get over there. Deza will make my day miserable if I show up too late."

"I'd actually enjoy seeing that." He laughed as I pushed his back.

We walked out into the dismal day and walked in the sand toward the conference room just down the beach a little way. I held up my half-eaten sandwich and smirked.

"This is really good. You wanna be my bitch for the next few weeks?"

"Yeah, sign me up for that shit." He rolled his eyes and opened the door, moving in and dusting off his tennis shoes. I hadn't bothered with shoes at all.

Deza stood in the far corner on her phone, bitching at someone about a bill we'd gotten that wasn't ours to pay.

I turned to find Frank explaining something to Riley. She had her back to me, and the way her tight white shorts fit her ass left my body screaming for far more attention than Vanessa had given it the night before. Poor girl. They always had such high aspirations only to fall flat on their faces.

After shoving the rest of my sandwich into my mouth, I walked over to stand beside Riley.

She glanced up and gave me a once-over before turning her attention back to Frank.

"So we're going to do the scene a few times and then work with other actors to critique each other?" She tilted her head to the side as he nodded. "Why? Why not just have me and Ethan work through it together over and over?"

"Because you think you're great and I think I'm great, and when we're together, we see no faults in our performance, but if I have to stand back and watch you, I'll see everything you don't. Vice versa." I pressed my shoulder to hers. "Good morning."

"Morning." She didn't look at me. Great. She was moody. Surely she wasn't on her period. Didn't the poor girl know that wearing white on her period was just a recipe for disaster?

"Ethan is right. It's the way we roll." Frank handed each of us a script. "This is a fight scene where you're pissed that Ethan is going back to his wife. It's the climax of the movie and we want it to be spot on emotionally. We'll be working on it today for as long as we need to. Read over the lines and get into position when you're ready."

"Sexual harassment. Did you get that on tape?" I glanced around and smiled, trying to lighten the mood.

Riley turned and walked toward the other side of the room without a word. I lifted my eyebrow and motioned toward her as I watched Frank closely.

"What's wrong with her?" I whispered.

He shrugged. "She was fine before you showed up. I'd assume you did something yesterday. Recount your afternoon and evening. You'll find it."

I rolled my eyes and turned my attention on the scene. It was short, but high emotion. I was almost too tired to muster up the anger the scene called for, but after diving into my shitty night with Vanessa I could feel the tension growing deep inside of me.

"I'm ready." I tossed the papers to the side and walked to the center of the moderate-sized conference room. "Riley?"

"Yep." She set her papers on the table beside Deza and walked towards me.

"All right. Get in places," Frank spoke louder than necessary.

Damn directors and their megaphone voices.

Riley put her hands on her hips and narrowed her eyes a little.

"Hot," I whispered and winked at her.

She didn't flinch. Damn... she was pissed, and it was my fault. I guess leaving her on the beach by herself the night before was a dick move. I was good at those. Apologizing on the other hand had never been a strong suit of mine.

"And action."

She pushed at my chest as her face contorted in anger. "I've given you all I have to offer. My time, my money, my attention, my body, my fucking heart." She pushed me harder, causing me to stumble backwards, which wasn't in the script.

I reached for her hands and grasped her wrists tightly, pulling her close to me and glaring down at her.

"And you'll keep giving it to me until I'm done using it." I leaned down and pressed my nose to hers as I growled softly, "You're mine. I don't care if you run a million miles from this place. You'll always be mine."

She jerked back, pulled her hand from mine and slapped me - hard.

"You're going back to her and you expect me to stay beside you? To keep your fucking bed warm while you live another life?" Tears swam in her eyes, and part of me couldn't tell where the drama began and she ended. She was so far into the character that I was forced to go farther with her.

"You'll do what I need you to do, Stacey." I licked my lips and gripped the sides of her beautiful face as tears dripped down her cheeks.

"Because you'll force me to? To love you from the sidelines forever?" The tears rolled down her cheeks and broke my heart. Was she trying to tell me something? No. They were lines.

I blinked a few times and stepped back. "I need a moment."

"What? Why?" Frank called out as I turned and walked out of the building and toward the water.

I had to get my shit together. I was a basket case most days as it were, but with her standing in front of me, forcing me to be better, more convincing, I was lost.

"Ethan?" Her voice caused me to turn.

"You okay?" She stopped in front of me and wiped at her eyes.

I reached out and brushed a tear away and nodded. "Yeah. Just trying to forgive myself for being a dick last night. I guess it's not my own forgiveness I want though."

"Well, you'll not be getting mine." She patted the side of my face. "Come on. Stop being a tit and let's get this scene down."

"I hate you," I mumbled and cupped her hand on my cheek, turning and kissing her palm softly. "You smell good."

"I masturbated with that hand this morning." We both laughed as she stepped back and shook her head. "Get in here and stop being so sensitive. I'm fine. I hate you, but we're good. Let's go."

I walked behind her, my heart racing, my mind running sprints around the possibilities of what it would feel like to let myself have a normal relationship, one where love and lust took turns. One where I could be me and give margin for her to simply be her.

It was a pipe dream that I needed to get over. She was authentic and real, and I was just me... America's favorite fake.

Chapter 16

Riley

I walked ahead of him, breathing through my mouth as I tried to slow my racing heart. The man had a way of making me feel a million emotions all at one time. I'd been waiting for the big break I had right in front of me for most of my life. I couldn't let something as silly as wanting Ethan's attention take anything away from that. He was as inaccessible with me standing in front of him as he was trapped behind the large movie screen as we all sat at the theater.

"You guys okay?" Deza met me at the door and backed up as I nodded and walked in.

"We both just slept like shit last night." I rolled my shoulders and moved to the center of the room.

"Maybe if you would just sleep together and get it over with, you'd both feel better." Paul turned from the coffee pot and shrugged. "Just saying. If we're keeping it real like you guys always do around here. There's sexual tension between you and the big cheese. Let it go, or give in to it."

I couldn't help but let my mouth fall open a little.

"Shut up, Paul. Jealous fucker." Ethan moved to stand in front of me and winked. "He's an idiot. You'll get used to him. His mom was a porn star and his dad a janitor with a love of anything with a pole attached to it. Brooms, mops, his mom."

I laughed and pressed my hand over my mouth.

"Good one. You get a point there, buddy." Paul laughed and crossed his free arm over his chest as he took a drink of his coffee.

"All right. Let's go, you two. Keep the emotion high. Okay?" Frank circled us and reached out and squeezed both of our shoulders. "You're in love and you're hiding it. Ethan, you're torn like a mother fucker on being with the woman you love and the one you've committed your life to in marriage."

"Got it." Ethan's warm brown eyes moved across my face, stealing another piece of my heart. "What are you thinking about when you cry on cue?"

"Lots of things." I swallowed hard and positioned myself as Frank barked out our cue to start. If I'd been honest, I would have told him that my tears were a direct correlation to knowing that he'd come close to being real with me the night before and backed off. That he'd decided to go find a whore in town to fuck throughout the night instead of sitting on the beach with me and getting to know each other better.

Nothing hurt more than rejection. At least not in my world. I'd suffered it too many times to let the wound heal. It was opened back up and made fresh far too often.

We worked through the scene several times before Frank called in a guy named Marco and a girl named Vanessa. Ethan's whole demeanor changed when the woman walked into the room.

"Fuck," he mumbled and walked back toward the snack table Deza had set up sometime during the day.

"What's up?" I moved over to stand beside him.

"That's the chick I took home with me last night. I had no clue she was an extra, but she knew." He ran his hand through his hair and glanced over his shoulder. "This is why I hate being me most days. Every decision seems like a bad one."

I couldn't help but rub salt in the wound a little. "Didn't you just tell me yesterday that sleeping with a random stranger was the quickest way to get your ass in trouble?"

"Yeah, I did." He crossed his arms over his chest as his expression darkened a little. I didn't want a fight, but there was no way in hell he was getting away with being a hypocrite and me not calling him on the floor for it.

"And then you go and do it?" I glanced over at her as she watched us. She was gorgeous with thick black hair and almond-colored skin. Her curves were thick and she had a good twenty pounds of sexiness stacked on her from where I stood. I couldn't come close to comparing. I felt like a pubescent boy with her in the room.

"You don't know what it's like to be alone, Riley. You have people in your life. Go judge someone else, all right?" He turned and walked toward Frank. "Let's do this shit. I'm ready for a nap."

"I know exactly what it's like, asshole." I moved up beside him and turned my attention on Marco. "Let's go first and show them how it's done?"

He chuckled and moved up to the center of the room. He looked like a male version of Vanessa. Charlotte would have a fucking cow if we ran into someone as good looking as him in the mall. Was everyone in the movies so well put together, and if so, did I really belong?

"Get into position," Frank barked from beside Ethan.

I winked at him and he smiled before locking his expression into surprised anger.

I pushed at his chest and let my anger for Ethan and his shitty decisions fuel me forward. "I've given you all I have to offer. My time, my money, my attention, my body, my fucking heart."

He gripped my hands and pulled me in tightly, locking my hands beside his thighs and glaring down at me. His dark features made him even more attractive, and yet he wasn't Ethan.

"And you'll keep giving it to me until I'm done using it." He leaned down and brushed his nose by mine as he took a step forward, which pressed us even closer. "You're mine. I don't care if you run a million miles from this place. You'll always be mine."

I jerked back and popped him in the face softly, trying not to overdo it. We were just rehearsing.

"You're going back to her and you expect me to stay beside you? To keep your fucking bed warm while you live another life?" I thought of my mother leaving me alone to raise myself, my father dying on us, Derick's bloody body being dropped on the front door and me finding him. Tears blurred my vision. The image of Ethan making love to the beautiful woman just behind Marco was the rest of the fuel I needed to dive into despair. I was alone. I'd always been alone. Now was no different. A sob left me that wasn't part of the script.

"You'll do what I need you to do, Stacey." He gripped the sides of my face and leaned down as tears dripped down my cheeks and I let out another soft sob.

"Because you'll force me to? To love you from the sidelines forever?" The tears rolled down my cheeks as I pressed up and closed my eyes, putting my heart into the kiss. All the broken pieces I could collect and offer.

"Cut." Ethan's voice surprised me. "We're not doing the kiss too, right?"

"No," Frank whispered and wiped at his eyes. "Shit. That was beautiful, Riley. Great job Marco. Very, very good."

I wiped at my eyes as Frank moved up and ran his hands down my shoulders. "That was beautiful. So much pain in your performance. You okay?"

I nodded as another wave of tears filled my eyes. "Yeah. Just trying to pull off the impossible."

"Well, you're doing it beautifully." He moved back and called Ethan and Vanessa up to run through the scene. I turned and walked out of the building. I knew Frank wanted me there to watch and take notes, but I needed a minute to get myself together.

I walked out to the edge of the water and slipped my hands into the back of my pockets and let out a long sigh. Ethan was so wrong about me. I knew more than anyone else what it felt like to be alone. He was a cocky bastard for thinking that he was the only one that suffered through life's tsunamis. He was one of many, and it would seem that most of his heartache was self-inflicted.

"Riley? You want to run the scene once more before we break for an hour?" Frank called down to me.

"You bet." I wiped at my eyes and jogged back up to the conference room.

Ethan and Vanessa were arguing in the corner when I walked back in, but I ignored them.

Marco moved up beside me and smiled. "You did great. So passionate."

"Thank you. Do you have a part in the movie?"

"Yeah. I play Ethan's brother." He shrugged. "It's fun. I love being on set no matter what part I have. One day I'll make it to the front of the stage."

"I think that day is coming sooner than you think." I smiled and moved toward the center of the room as he grasped my wrist and stopped me.

"Riley. You wanna maybe go out for a drink while you're here this week?" His eyes moved across my face.

"Yeah. That sounds fun. Maybe after we get through the first few days of filming. I'm so new to this that I don't want to mess anything up." I gave him a sheepish smile that wasn't at all my personality.

"Sounds great. You just let me know when." He winked and moved back beside Frank.

"Let him know when what?" Ethan moved to stand in front of me. The pink stain on his cheeks and neck let me know that he was struggling. Vanessa wasn't going to let him live down whatever happened with them the night before. I almost felt sorry for him. Almost.

"He just wants to get a drink."

"Tell him no." Ethan glanced over at Frank. "Let's do this. I need a drink."

"Don't tell me what to do." I tugged at his t-shirt. "Focus and stop being an ass."

"You're not getting a drink with him." He gave me a tight, asinine smile as Frank yelled action.

We moved through it with intense anger until we reached the slap. I hit him harder than I had Marco, but not nearly as hard as I had the first time.

"You're going back to her and you expect me to stay beside you? To keep your fucking bed warm while you live another life?" I half-screamed with emotion so real it ripped open my heart.

"You'll do what I need you to do, Stacey." He gripped the sides of my face and leaned down as tears dripped down my cheeks.

"Because you'll force me to? To love you from the sidelines forever?" I searched his eyes for the truth of his answer.

He moved in like a snake, striking hard as he pressed his lips to mine. The world disappeared as I wrapped my arms around his waist and lifted up, meeting his passion with something blistering hot - my own need to belong to him.

He pressed his tongue deep into my mouth, and I turned my head and opened up, sucking hard as I dug my fingers into the top of his ass and groaned into his mouth.

He deepened the kiss and jerked me farther against him. I could almost hear Frank speaking, but nothing mattered.

His fingers brushed down the side of my neck as he broke the kiss and pressed his head to mine, panting softly.

"I want you so fucking bad," he whispered and went in for another kiss.

By the time we pulled apart, the room was empty and emotion rolled over me in a way that left me crippled.

"I'm going to my room." I turned and half-stumbled to the door as tears burned my eyes. I wanted that passion in my life more than I wanted my brother back. More than I wanted my mother to be a mother. More than I wanted my career to blossom into something that made me feel worthy.

I wanted him. Period.

Chapter 17

Four Days Later
Ethan

She wasn't herself for the rest of the week, or at least not the girl I'd come to know in a short period of time. Her cockiness had waned, her confidence dimmed. This odd need to protect her rolled over me about halfway through the week, and I had to try hard to pull myself back. What I thought was going to be a great time together ended up being awkward and tense.

By the weekend, I was worn the hell out.

"All right buddy. You're up for this one." Frank popped me on the back as I stood beside the scene they'd recreated of a beach party. Extras milled about everywhere, looking casual as if in the throes of an actual party on the beach. Riley was beside Deza and had her arms over her chest. The faraway look in her eyes haunted me.

"Right. Watch how it's done." I wagged my eyebrows and caught a glimpse of a smile from her. Deza rolled her eyes and motioned for me to get to it. It was almost time to break for the day.

Marco walked up to the bar and glanced back at me. "You ready, boss?"

"Yeah." I patted his back. I'd been an ass for most of the week to the guy because Riley seemed to find a friend in him. I had to get over myself. We had at least ten months of working together as a team. As childish as I wanted to be over him getting her attention, I couldn't jeopardize all we had going on.

"And action!" Frank yelled from the side of the scene.

I moved through the motions, talking with Marco for a few minutes and catching the eye of a few women. The creepy-looking guy who moved along the edge of the party slipped onto the scene, and I turned, letting him know that I was onto him. His sprint off the scene, and my own in following him left us done for the day.

"Great job." Frank smiled at me before moving up to talk to the extras.

"What are you girls up to for the rest of the day?" I slipped my hands into my pants pockets and made sure to eye both Deza and Riley.

"I'm going to read a good book on the beach. You?" Deza pulled off her sunglasses and cleaned them on her t-shirt.

"I'm not sure. I don't want to be alone. I know that." I glanced toward Riley. "How about you, pretty girl?"

"I'm not sure. I think I'll walk the beach and look for seashells. Charlotte collects them, so taking a few back to her would make up for being gone."

"Charlotte, as in Jade?" I smirked as she laughed. It was the first real emotion I'd seen from her in days. "Can I come with you?"

"Yeah. It's a free beach." She was back on lockdown. "I'm going to grab a coke. You want something?"

"I'll take one too. Thanks." I waited until she left to turn my heavy stare onto Deza. "All right. Spill. What the fuck is up with her? I didn't do anything. I promise." I lifted my hands as if in surrender.

"I know. She's struggling with keeping fantasy from reality. You know how hard that is. Remember your first love scene? You were so convinced that Trish was in love with you that you started looking at rings." She gave me a cheeky grin.

"I did not." I ran my fingers through my hair and glanced over to watch her talk with the bartender. "Does she think I'm in love with her?"

"Are you?"

"Is that a joke? I don't know what love is. I'm in lust with her for sure." I shrugged. "It's acting, D. It was a hard lesson for me to learn too, but she's got to separate it or her life is going to be far more hard than it should have to be."

"I agree." She reached out and ran her hand down my arm. "Coach her and help her understand how things work. You're the only actor here. I'm not capable of even beginning to understand where she's at."

"Is she in love with me?" Butterflies danced around my stomach at the thought.

"No, but she's hurt too easily by you just being you. She's sensitive because firstly, she's a young woman in a new world and two, she wants love like the rest of us do."

"Speak for yourself." I pulled my hands from my pockets. "I'll talk with her."

"Thank you." She moved back and left me standing there with my thoughts. My eyes moved across her as she walked toward me, but kept her eyes adverted toward the water. Her short strawberry-blond hair had a girlie curl at the ends of it, and her pink lipstick had me yearning to rub it off in the most unconventional of ways.

"Here you are, Mr. Lewis." She glanced up at me and smiled.

"Thanks, madam." I took the coke as she pulled her sunglasses into place. I hadn't noticed how impersonal she looked without the expression bleeding through her eyes. I almost asked her to take them off, but it seemed stupid. "You ready to go on this grand seashell hunting adventure?"

She took a long drink of her coke before moaning and nodded. "That I am."

I moved in behind her and pressed my hand to the front of my slacks. The sound of her voice was enough to call the beast from its slumber, but her sexy little moans would make sure he stayed alert just in case there was *any* hope of getting petted.

"Did you like the scene? The action ones are my favorite." I moved up beside her and couldn't help but to tilt my face toward her, so I could watch her more closely. From afar, she was gorgeous, but up close, she was quite capable of stealing hearts and ruining marriages.

"I did. Are you open for a word of criticism?" She took another sip of her drink and kept her face turned toward the ground. She knelt and dug a small shell from the sand.

"From you? Of course. I don't think anyone else's opinion would be welcomed." I knelt beside her and dug out another one.

"Why is mine welcomed?" She pulled her glasses to rest on top of her head and studied me.

"Because you're my partner in crime." I reached out and touched the tip of her nose. "And I value your opinion."

"If you stood closer to Marco during the opening of the scene, your relationship would look more plausible. It's an awkward gap at best." She shrugged. "My best friend and I always stand shoulder to shoulder. I know you're a dude, but Jace and his good friend Dane always stand side by side when they're together."

"Dane? Jace has a best friend named Dane?" I couldn't help but smirk.

"What's so funny about that?" Her defensiveness was on the rise.

"It's just cute." I shrugged, stood up and walked to the water to wash off the shell.

"Do you have something against Jace?"

"Yes. He's sleeping with the woman I want in my bed." I stood and turned, confessing without apology. I didn't care if she knew. If she didn't, she was far more dense than I imagined possible.

"What do you want from me, Ethan Lewis?" She moved to stand in front of me as her expression grew tight.

"For you to let your hair down and stop fighting against me. We're going to be doing this shit together for a long time. It doesn't have to be love, Riley. It can just be lust." I touched the side of her face, brushing my thumb over her bottom lip as my pulse quickened. I ached for a night with her. "It's not that involved. It can just be part of us taking care of each other."

"No, it can't." She gripped my hand and held on tightly as she glanced out toward the water. "Jace and I are fuck-buddies. I don't need another one in my life. He's doing the job just fine."

She was stabbing in the dark, hoping to hurt me.

I dropped my soda can and gripped the other side of her neck as I leaned in and brushed my nose by hers. "I don't doubt for a minute that he's living the high life with a beautiful woman like you in his bed, but are you? Are you sure you're not missing out on something explosive. Are you not interested at all?"

I locked eyes with her and enjoyed far too much watching her question herself.

"Do you agree about the positioning with you and Marco at the beginning of the scene?" She searched my face.

I laughed and nipped at her lips before releasing her. "I actually do. You're spot on with that, even if your transitions still suck donkey dick."

"You're so vulgar." She smiled and knelt down to pick up another shell.

"You're not at all curious if we would make a good couple in the bedroom?" I pressed my hand to the front of my slacks again, wishing I had control of my body around her.

"Of course I am." She glanced back at me, looking more like the woman that took care of me on the plane and less like the angry bitch that slapped me harder than was necessary at the beginning of the week. She had as many sides to her personality as I did. It was almost concerning.

"Then let me take you back to my room and make you writhe in pleasure. It's a release we could both use." I licked at my lips and tried to still my racing heart. The idea of getting her naked and memorizing every sweet curve of her body had my head spinning. As a man who could have any woman I wanted in the world, I wanted the one before me, and of course she was holding out.

"I have a fuck-buddy, Ethan. It's hard enough not to fall in love with him. I'm not playing the balancing game with you too." She stood up and walked down the beach away from me.

"Okay, fine. I think the day will come when we give in to each other, but until then, let's at least build up a tight friendship." I jogged to catch up with her.

"I'd like that. Just remember that it's just a friendship." She rolled her shoulders before lifting her hands to the sky. "Nothing more."

"A good working relationship too, right?" I poked her side, causing her to yelp and drop her hands. "We gotta pretend to be hot for each other during the scenes too."

"I'm aware of that. I can fake just about anything." She gave me a cute smile that had me thinking along the same lines as she'd spoken moments before. How easy it would be to seduce her and let lust bleed into love. It was a fucking scary thought, and yet one that seemed to linger as we continued down the beach.

"Are you really still thinking about graduating from UCLA?" I slipped my hands in my pockets and kicked at a patch of seaweed.

"That was the worst transition I have ever seen." She laughed and pushed me from the side with her shoulder.

I laughed. "Yes, that was horrible. My train of thought went from licking every inch of you to what you planned to do when we get back. Then I realized that you were still in school. You mentioned mid-terms, and I thought, damn... I couldn't manage all that. I wondered how you were doing with it, and if you really planned on finishing."

She stopped and knelt again as laughter rose up around her. "You're incorrigible."

"What?" I knelt beside her and pushed, knocking her over.

"You ass." She reached out and pulled me down with her.

I moved onto my side and reached out, running my fingers along her arm as she turned on her side to face me.

"What was incorrigible about asking you if you were graduating?"

"Not that part." She sat up and pulled her knees to her chest, leaving plenty of leg for me to stare at. I had to remember to send a thank you note to her momma for teaching her to wear shorty-shorts. The bottom curve of her ass peeked out as she shifted and looked out at the water.

"What part?" I pressed my teeth into my bottom lip and forced myself to look back up at her face.

"About licking every inch of me." She was a little breathless. I loved it.

I reached out and ran the back of my fingers down the back of her thigh, curving along her exposed flesh.

She stiffened beside me. "Ethan."

"I do want to lick every inch of you." I licked my lips and moved up to sit beside her. "I wanna know how you taste. It's driving me nuts."

"You're such a whore." She laughed.

I wrapped an arm around her shoulder and pressed my lips to the side of her head. "It's lonely being a whore by yourself. Be one with me?"

Her laughter made the moment. Something told me that my desire for sex was just a safe way to ask for more. I'd never given myself to anyone in a relationship outside of Deza and Liam. Feeling her worm her way deep inside of me was frightening and thrilling all at the same time.

Chapter 18

Riley

We'd parted ways after a few more minutes together, which was for the better. I was close to agreeing to just about anything he wanted. The goal was to build my career and give Mr. Ethan Lewis a good dose of reality, but it seemed like he was pulling me into fantasy instead.

The text I got shortly after getting back to my room and flopping down on the bed was a request for me to have dinner with him. I laughed at the thought of him trying to get through dinner without hitting on me, talking about his greatness or moving the conversation toward his cock in some manner or form. The guy's modesty hadn't seen the light of day - ever.

I shot him a note back that I'd be in the kitchen at six and we could grab something to eat. After laying down the rules about the evening, I curled up in the bed and let my mind go wild. I'd not been daydreaming about what the night would have looked like if we were lovers in an old-fashioned movie for more than ten minutes when Deza walked in.

"You awake?" she whispered.

I rolled over and sat up. "Yeah. Just thinking."

"Everything all right?" She dropped down on the edge of her bed and ran her hands over her hair.

"Yeah. They're good. I'm excited about filming the boat scene next week. I love being out on the water." I propped myself up on my elbow and studied her. "You okay? You look like something is wrong."

"I'll be all right." She lay back and let out a long sigh. "I just wish I could figure out how to get Darren to trust me again. It's been ten damn years. It was a mistake to sleep with Zane. I know that now. Hell, I knew that then."

"Have you talked to him about it?"

"A million times." She turned over and crawled up into her bed. "He won't listen to me. He thinks that once trust is broken, that's it. There is no getting it back."

"Do you believe that?" I pulled the covers around me and snuggled under them, wishing I had some advice to share. I was nothing but a kid with a dream and very little positive life experience to back it up. There were days when I was surprised that I wasn't beside my mother, living the hard life in the midst of drugs and whatever else she'd gotten herself into.

"I don't know to be honest. I'd like to think I'm the kind of person that would give another person a chance if they fucked up, but I don't know if I would. Trust is such a delicate thing, you know? One lie can break it all apart."

I nodded, but kept silent. My lie about Jace was weighing heavy on me. I'd come clean with Ethan at the beach an hour before, but it still felt like a shitty move on my part. Compounding that was the lie about testing him in his kitchen during our first mentor meeting. He shouldn't trust me at all, and yet I knew that he did. He planned on the two of us protecting each other for a long time to come.

"Maybe I should just let it go." Deza's voice softened, lost steam.

"No." I sat up and brushed my hands over my hair. "No. You don't let it go. If you love him, you fight for it. He's worth fighting for, right?"

"Absolutely." She pressed her palms to her face. "You're right. I haven't been fighting. I've been tiptoeing around the edges of our fucked up relationship. I need to dive in deep and risk it all. Maybe then he'll see me for who I really am. I'm a good person. I was young and dumb."

"He'll see it. He's old and dumb now." I smiled as she chuckled. "Go all in. The worst thing that can happen is that you're rejected and then you get over it. You heal and finally move on."

"Have you always been an old soul?" She sat up and pulled her phone from her pocket. "I'm going to go call him while I have the nerve to do it."

"Good. I've got my fingers crossed." I moved to the edge of the bed and pressed my hands against my knees. "Deza."

She stood and turned to face me. "What?"

"I know you don't want to hear this, but I'm honestly considering Ethan's proposal for us to take care of each other."

"I think that's awesome. You guys are going to have to bind together. These films get harder and harder. Taking advice from the other and working to make sure-" She paused and tilted her head a little. "Wait a minute. Like protect each other or like... take *care* of each other."

"Both." I rolled my shoulders in and held my breath, waiting for the ass chewing.

"I see. Well, you're a woman. You know the consequences of giving yourself over to someone only to have the possibility of them rejecting you the next time. Ethan is a fickle creature. Just make sure if you decide to be stupid, and let's get this straight, I think you guys are being quite stupid, that you keep your heart out of the mix. He's an ass in the bedroom because of his issues."

"His issues?" I stood up as my stomach sickened. Why had I brought up my thoughts to sleep with Ethan with his agent? She and I were growing closer, but there was still a defined line between us. She wasn't my agent yet, even though she was taking care of me much better than Darren ever had.

"His size." She put her hands on her hips. "Don't tell me you haven't noticed."

"Why in the world would that be an issue? Men would pay millions of dollars to have what he has." Confusion raced through me. Was there more to the story that I wasn't getting access too?

"Yeah but, not that big." She let out a soft sigh. "Everyone sees what they want to see, Riley. I don't want Ethan to think I was talking about his personal life behind his back. He's like family to me. I'm just saying that he's way too big for most women, and he's incredibly frustrated because of it. It's not a joke or a positive scenario for him. He takes a huge risk every time he takes off his clothes. I honestly couldn't do that to myself if it were me."

"Wow." I sat back down on the edge of the bed. "It's that big of a deal."

"Absolutely. He's incredibly sensitive about it." She shrugged. "Do what you think is best, but you're going to have to understand that if you guys try each other on for size, the chances of that turning out as anything positive are slim to none."

I sat in silence, but nodded as she turned and walked out of the room. I couldn't remember having had a more awkward conversation in my whole life, and I'd been involved in a few doozies during my teenage years.

The conversation with Ethan over the size of his cock raced through my mind. He'd been so different after I teased him about it. I'd assumed he was just having another one of his emotional imbalances that he seemed prone to. That wasn't it at all.

Pulling out my phone, I pulled up his bio again and lay back on the bed. I had an hour before I needed to start getting ready for dinner and wanted to know more about him. If we were going to be friends or lovers or both, I needed to better understand who he was as a person. Who the man behind the mask was, and if I cared about him, or just one of the many faces he wore.

A host of emotions assaulted me as I finished putting on a little bit of make-up for our dinner. The white dress I'd chosen was flirty and fun, a little too sexy maybe, but I didn't care. After reading about Ethan's parents pimping him out as a kid and moving across the world on the money he'd made without worrying much about him and Liam after that, I was heartbroken for him.

He'd been raised by his grandmother on his mother's side, and his bio had so many great things to say about the woman. She'd died when he was sixteen, but by then, he was with Deza, living the life he thought would help him find wholeness. I couldn't force myself to read any more as my heart was already filled to the brim with his honesty in the book, his openness.

"I wanna know that guy so badly." I brushed my thumb under my bottom lip and cleaned up my lipstick a little.

A knock at the door surprised me. I checked my hair one more time and opened the door to find Ethan standing there with a single yellow lily in his hand. His white polo looked good against his tanned skin. The dark blue shots he wore gave him a casual and yet dressy appeal all at the same time.

"You ready?" He pressed his hand to the door as his eyes moved down the front of my dress. "Damn, you're so far beyond fine."

"Thank you?" I laughed and snagged the flower from him. "Is this for me?"

"Nope. It was for Deza. She here?" He winked and moved back to let me out. "You in the mood for sushi? I found a place about half a mile down the beach. There might be adoring fans there, but I'll make sure to beat them off of you all right?"

I laughed again, finding a warmth beside him that I was almost frightened to find. We didn't know anything about each other and yet there was a comfort that permeated our relationship if I allowed it. It was the angst of lust that blurred the lines.

"I love sushi. And in all honesty, if we get bombarded by a group of raging mad women with lust in their eyes and saliva dripping from their jowls, then I'll protect you." I moved closer to him as we walked down the hall toward the stairs.

"Wow. That was... dramatic." He chuckled and opened the door to the back exit of the house. "Did the ones the other day have a drooling problem?"

"Most women do around you, silly. You're Ethan Lewis... America's heartthrob."

He gave me a look that said he wasn't at all happy with the title. "Can I just be Ethan tonight? Mr. Lewis went to bed early with a headache and a hangover."

"Too much liquor and sex?" I teased him as we stepped out onto the sand.

"Yep. He's a bastard, that guy... I tell you what. I'm surprised he has a friend in the world."

"Well, he has me." I lifted the flower to my nose and let the moment settle on me. My words were true. He did have me.

Chapter 19

Ethan

She looked like an angel in her dress and dainty brown sandals. It was going to be a long night of keeping myself in check. The fact that she was being sweet was gnawing at the part of me that wanted romance and love over sweaty hot shower sex. That guy was still there too, but he was getting sucker punched by the toga-wearing cupid inside my chest.

"So tell me a little more about your school program. Are you graduating with drama as your major, or did you go a different route?" I wanted to take her hand, but it would be too intimate. I'd ruin the evening later for sure with a dumb-ass move. I'd hold off as long as I could until then.

She glanced over at me, stealing my breath. "I'm a drama major. I thought I might go into international business, but I just couldn't force myself to give up on my dreams of acting one day." She shrugged. "I figured I would graduate in May with my degree and change agents. If I could score the right one, I might have the chance to get in front of the right people and yadda yadda. You know the drill, I'm sure."

"Sure do." I slipped my hands into my pockets as we approached the restaurant. "Are you guys doing a spring production, or is that just something the movies make up about drama departments in college?"

I was ignorant to most things outside of the acting business only because I'd been suffocated by it for all of my adult life, and most of my childhood. I held the door and followed behind her, wishing we were a couple so I could touch her as freely as I wanted to. I was a guy without patience for easing into anything. It was a head-first dive off the tallest diving board available for me, regardless of what lay below.

She waited to answer until we were seated across from each other at an intimate table in the back.

"We are doing a play in a few weeks. I'm the lead for it this time, which is exciting, and yet so overshadowed by what you guys are giving me the opportunity to do." Her smile was contagious. The sarcastic, quick-witted woman that had my cock acting like a fit-throwing child for attention was tucked away somewhere.

Funny enough, it didn't seem to matter which side of her I got to experience, my body demanded the naked side. I smirked at the thought, but covered it up by glancing at the waitress and ordering a bottle of wine.

"Wait. Are you... Oh my God. You're Ethan Lewis."

"Nope," Riley spoke up. "He just looks like him. We get that all the time, don't we, baby?"

My cock twitched at her words. I'd have rolled my eyes at myself if I could have gotten away with it.

"That's right, sweetheart. You're just a lucky girl to have found a body double for that big, sexy hunk." I wagged my eyebrows.

The server laughed, and Riley rolled her eyes dramatically enough for the both of us. I laughed as the server walked off and Riley gave me a look.

There was my girl under the sweet smile and the light covering of make-up.

"Really? You're so full of shit." Her grimace turned into a smile as she laughed and sat back. "Are you going to come see my spring production?"

"Do you want me to?" I pulled my napkin in my lap and let my eyes move down to the sweet swell of her breasts just above the top of her strapless dress. I wanted to brush my lips by her exposed skin and drown in the sound of her begging for more.

"Yeah. That would be pretty cool." She wagged her eyebrows. "I mean... can you imagine it? Me? Little old, nobody of a person, me having the biggest actor of our time come sit in the auditorium at UCLA to support me?"

"You're not a nobody." My smile faded. "Don't say that again. I don't like it."

Her smiled faded too. "Okay. I'm just saying."

"Well, don't. I'm no different than you. You're somebody's something special, I'm sure. Hell, I'm fighting like a madman to make sure you don't end up mine." I tried to play my words off as being cheeky, but the realization that rushed across her pretty face told me that I was caught.

"Anyways," she whispered and glanced down at her lap. "It's going to be a fun play. The only hard part is having to kiss the male lead. He's not at all someone I would look at twice."

"So shallow." I winked at her and enjoyed the power I had to make her smile again.

"You're telling me that you've never struggled having to kiss someone in a movie that you weren't turned on by?" She moved her forearms up to rest on the table. Her position pressed her breasts together and lifted them even more.

My body throbbed with need as I swallowed hard. If we ever ended up naked, I'd have to see if she'd let me press myself between her pretty tits and-

"Are you still with me?" She lifted her eyebrow and smirked.

I swallowed hard and reached for my water as embarrassment rolled over me. I would normally have just told her what I was thinking, but it seemed almost too crass to speak out loud. What the fuck was wrong with me?

"Yep. Just thinking about all the times I've kissed someone on screen and had to fake the shit out of the passion." I shrugged. "When I was younger it was easier to do and still enjoy. Kissing a woman at seventeen or eighteen when you don't find her attractive is still kissing a woman. I can't remember the last time I got turned on when acting until you showed up."

She leaned back in her chair and dropped her hands to her lap. "And why were you turned on by me?"

"Are you kidding me? You look like a movie star from the early days of film. Back when women still wore enough clothing to tease a man into seduction and forced him to bed to see what was under the nightie. Now it's almost as if the action movie with one sex scene is a porn in disguise." I gave a look of disgust. "It's not at all what I would do if it were up to me."

"I'm honestly a little surprised to hear this." She picked up her wine glass and took a drink as our server poured us each a glass.

"Why's that? Just because I'm vulgar on occasion, want to get you in bed as much as I want my next check from Eon and offered you sex a few times? Psh. That's nothing. I'm still a classy guy under all that drama."

"Are you?" She tilted her head to the side, causing her hair to drape over her shoulder seductively.

"Very much so." I nodded toward the lily. "I brought you a flower tonight, right?"

"That's for Deza, remember?"

I chuckled. Cheeky little bitch. She was going to steal my heart while I was trying to steal her panties to add to my collection.

"What's this guy look like that you're unwilling to kiss?"

"That was a horrible transition."

"Yes, I'm quite aware. Tell me anyway. I don't like him already, so describe him and give me a reason to feel sorry for him." I picked up my menu and pointed to a few sushi rolls that Riley agreed on sharing with me.

"He's okay, but he's terribly thin and honestly he lacks confidence. He'd be a good-looking guy if he just squared his shoulders and lifted his chin." She jerked her shoulders back and lifted her chin.

"Mmmm... do that again for me." I sucked my bottom lip into my mouth as my body started to pulse in all the right places.

"You're corrupt." She crossed her arms over her chest and shook her head. "And here I thought maybe there was a good-guy side to you."

"Oh, there is." I smiled. "He's just the facade for the real me."

"The you that wants to have a friends with benefits relationship with your new co-star. A relationship that could potentially ruin everything between us."

"Or." I lifted my finger. "Or it could make it even better. Can you imagine if we had a kissing scene tomorrow after you let me spend the night making you wonder how in the fuck you ever survived without me pressed to the front of you?"

"I like it from behind." She shrugged and picked up her glass.

The blood drained from my face, my chest, my legs, my arms, leaving me numb. Every bit of energy I had rushed toward my cock and brought the fucker raging to life. I took a quick breath and nodded.

"Good. I like it any way you're willing to give it." I licked at my lips. "Let's get out of here."

"No. Behave." She smiled and moved back as the soup was delivered. Why we'd decided to have dinner instead of just staying at the house and having me cook for her was beyond me. I sucked like hell at cooking, but for her... for the chance to experience her... I was willing to try.

Chapter 20

Riley

The air was so damn hard to breathe as we worked our way through the rest of dinner. We moved the conversation back to my time at UCLA and talked a little about Liam too. I tried to stay away from anything that might give him the ability to flirt too much. I was already raw from reading his bio, then getting the flower and now having him watch me like an animal might its favorite prey.

My body was heated, my pulse spiked to the point of discomfort, but like any good actress, I put on a mask and made it through dinner.

"You ready?" He smiled and got up, moving around to help me out of my chair.

"Absolutely. That was fantastic." I took his hand and moved behind him out of the restaurant. It was comical how many times I heard his name whispered as we moved out the back door and back into the sand.

"We should practice your kissing scene with Mr. Less-than-Confident. That way when you go to do it, you can close your eyes and see me instead." He kept my hand tightly in his.

Indecision tore up my insides on whether to pull it from him, or just go with the flow.

"Why do you need fans when you have yourself?" I laughed and pulled him to a stop. I tugged my hand from his and reached down to undo my sandals. He snagged them from me and gripped my hand again.

"I like how confident you are... you don't like that about me?" He glanced down at me and the world seemed to stop. I was in trouble. So much trouble, not because of who he was, but the simple power he had over me.

"I like a lot of things about you," I whispered and released his hand to jog down the beach. "Come on, old man. Catch up."

"You know this should be a scene in a movie." He jogged behind me. "Except you should be running toward me, not away from me."

I laughed and let the warmth of the ocean breeze race over my skin, taking me away to a place where everything was all right. I didn't have to pretend to be or not be anyone. I could just let myself go and enjoy life for the moment.

"This isn't a movie." I turned and lifted my arms to the side as I panted softly. "It's real life. It's a good life. It's the life I want."

"You're making me want it." He tossed my shoes to the side and pulled his shirt over his shoulders, tossing it too.

"Ethan. What are you doing?" I reached out to stop him from crashing into me.

"Taking what I want." His mouth covered mine as he wrapped his arms around me tightly and took me down to the sand below.

I groaned and pressed my foot into the wet sand to roll us. "No. Honestly. I won't be able to survive you."

"Is it my size?" His eyes filled with worry as he lay beneath me on the sand. The moon left the scene far too romantic.

"What? No." I leaned down and ran my fingers through the top of his hair before kissing him again.

He rolled us and pressed me to the cold earth below, licking and sucking at my mouth before moving down to press his teeth against the side of my neck.

"Come to bed with me. Let me make you feel things you could only dream of." His breath was hot against my ear, his body so big and solid against mine. I felt protected, desired, beloved. It was a lie, but I wanted to drown in it as long as I could.

"I can't," I whispered and opened my legs farther as he reached down and pulled my skirt up my legs. He shifted his hips and ground against me as we both groaned loudly.

"Yeah, you can, Riley. I'm not going to hurt you. I'm an asshole to almost everyone else, but I wouldn't do that to you. Let's try each other out and if it doesn't work, go back to Jace, but if we end up being everything I know we could be... fuck." He licked my ear and moved up to press his lips back against mine.

I tilted my head a little and opened up, letting him in deeply as he aggressively rocked against me and made love to my mouth. I'd never felt so much passion. The buildup was orgasmic alone.

"Let me in," he murmured against my mouth and slid his hands around my hips to grip my ass tight as he squeezed and licked at the soft skin under my ear. "I want deep inside of you, Riley. Don't deny me. You don't want to."

And I didn't. Not in the slightest.

I cried out as his fingers slipped into the bottom of my panties and brushed by my sex. I knew how sloppy wet I was, but embarrassment wouldn't come.

"So wet. I knew you wanted me too." He sucked my earlobe into his mouth and petted me softly as he grunted and rocked into me.

I would never have believed in a million years that I'd be on a beach pressed beneath Ethan Lewis had someone told me that was the future. Never. It was a dream come true, and yet nightmares played behind my eyes.

"Ethan." I panted against the salty skin of his neck. "Not here."

"No?" He moved back and pushed against the sand to sit up on his knees. "Come to my room then."

"You know this isn't going to end well."

He stood and pulled me up before picking me up. I yelped and smacked him in the chest.

"It's going to end with both of us coming like fountains. I'm thinking that's the goal in sex, right?" He kissed me again as my body purred for him.

"Yeah. That's the goal." I touched the side of his face and shifted to kiss him again.

He got us inside and set me down outside of his room. We were covered in sand and salt water, both looking like hell, and yet neither of us cared.

I slid my hands around his waist and cupped his cock, stroking him hard as I pressed my breasts against his back and my teeth into the thick meat of his back.

"I want you so goddamn bad my hands are shaking." He laughed before moaning and fumbling with the lock on the door.

"Me too. Hurry the hell up." I cupped his balls and licked up his spine as something burst open inside of me. I was giving myself to him and whatever the fallout looked like... fuck it. I would deal with it.

"There." He opened the door and turned to grab me, pulling me roughly against him as someone else grabbed me from behind.

"Hey. Sorry kids." Frank.

It was as if I'd been dunked in ice water. I yelped and moved into the room behind Ethan. My white dress was translucent at that point, and there wasn't much to hide.

"What the fuck, Frank? Get out, dude. Shit." Ethan was hot. Pissed in a way I wasn't sure I was comfortable with.

"I'm sorry. Seriously, but Riley left her cell phone here earlier. It's been going off nonstop. It's from LA. Just check it and make sure everything is okay." He handed it to Ethan and walked off.

"Here. Check it out while I run us some bath water. I wanna wash you up before I take my time getting intimate with every inch of you." He touched the side of my face and leaned down to kiss me hard once.

I breathed him in and moved back as he ducked into the bathroom.

The calls were from Charlotte. What the hell could be so important to blow up my phone over and over again?

I listened to them as each one got more frantic. I dropped down on the bed and pressed the phone to my ear as my heart beat so hard I grew faint. The last one was enough to make my food finish its trip up my chest and force me to run for the toilet to lose my dinner. I had to get home. Now.

The sound of her voice echoed in the bathroom around me as Ethan's strong hands pulled my hair from my face. He whispered words of comfort, but I couldn't seem to hear or feel anything other than her voice in my ear as the last message played over the speakerphone.

"Riley! Pick up the goddamn phone. Pick up." Crying. So much sobbing. Heart wrenching sobs. "It's your mom. She's... she's been in an accident. I'm at the hospital, Riley. I need you to get home. I don't know what to do." She sobbed a little more before the sound of muffled voices filled the line and Charlotte's soft scream bled into another round of sobs. "Oh fuck. She didn't make it. Riley. You need to come home. Your mom... your mom didn't make it."

Want More?

Understudy, Book 3 continues the story...

About the Author

Ali Parker is a full-time contemporary romance writer who is looking to flood the market this year with lots of great, quick reads. She loves coffee, watching a great movie and handing out with her hubs. By hanging out, she means making out. Hanging out is for those little creepy elves at Christmas. No tight green stockings for her.

www.aliparkerbooks.com

Also by Ali Parker

Baited
Second Chance Romances
Jaded
Justified
Judged
Alpha Billionaire Series
Alpha Billionaire, Book 1
Alpha Billionaire, Book 2
Together Forever
Bad Money Series
Blood Money
Dirty Money
Hard Money
Cash Money
Forbidden Fruit Series
Forgotten Bodyguard
Future Investment
Risky Business
Bright Lights Billionaire
Stage Left
Center Stage
Pro-U Series
Breakaway